SLEIGH BELL DREAMS

Mistletoe Meadows
Book 1

JESSIE GUSSMAN

Contents

Acknowledgments

Cover art by Covers and Cupcakes
Editing by Heather Hayden
Narration by Jay Dyess
Author Services by CE Author Assistant

Listen to the unabridged audio for FREE performed by Jay Dyess
on the Say with Jay channel on YouTube. Get early access to all of
Jay's recordings and listen to Jessie's books before they're
available to the general public, plus get daily Bible readings by
Jay and bonus scenes by becoming a Say with Jay channel
member.

Chapter One

"You're welcome to stay with me," Marjerie McBride said before a crash sounded in the background. "Hold on a second."

Terry McBride smiled as her mom must have slid the phone away from her mouth because her voice came from a distance as she said, "Children, I'm on the phone! You need to be quiet! And no running in the house!" She sighed, and her voice came back on the line. "I'm sorry about that."

"Mom. Things are crazy there right now. With Gilbert and Sally back, and Sally's cancer, and you watching their kids for them while they go for treatments, it's just too much."

"You're just as welcome here as they are. You're just as much my child."

"But I don't have three kids, and I don't have a wife with cancer. Gilbert needs you now," she said. "You and Dad did so much for me while I was in med school, and then in residency, you guys were awesome. I don't know anyone else who had parents who were as supportive and caring as you. You guys made sure I ate, for goodness' sake. You brought homemade food to me. I can't thank you enough."

"Just because we did stuff for you then does not mean that we're not ready to do stuff now."

"I know. But right now, it's Gilbert's turn. I can find something." Although she wasn't sure whether that was true. Her hometown, Mistletoe Meadows, seemed to be in somewhat of a housing crisis. She hadn't been able to find a single place for rent.

Maybe she just hadn't been looking in the right places.

"I don't know. I've heard that it's kind of hard to find a house right now. Have you even looked?"

"I've looked a little bit." She grimaced as she said that. That wasn't entirely true. She'd looked an awful lot and hadn't been able to find a thing, but she already decided that moving in with her mother was not going to happen.

"You need to start at the clinic on Monday. Didn't you say you had appointments?"

"I do, but I'm sure I'll find something." She hadn't wanted the clinic to stay closed too long. Dr. Vivik had closed it just a month before when he had retired unexpectedly due to his wife having cancer.

This was the opportunity of a lifetime for her. She'd always wanted to move back to her hometown, although she knew that it might not happen. Dr. Vivik was just in his early sixties, and she had at least another five years. Or so she thought.

But after his wife was diagnosed, her mom had gently suggested that perhaps he would like for Terry to come and take over, and Dr. Vivik had jumped at the chance.

She had had to give her current employer, a group of physicians she was with in Richmond, Virginia, notice, and she'd wanted to be fair. So she'd given them an entire month.

It had been a busy month as word of her departure got around and patients requested to see her one last time before she left.

She hadn't made it to Mistletoe Meadows to do more than meet with Dr. Vivik several times to discuss how he ran his office, and they'd discussed the fact that she would keep the same employees, if they would stay. There was one nurse and one receptionist.

It was a small town and a small, close-knit community, and the type of doctor's office that Dr. Vivik ran fit right in.

Terry intended it would be the same for her.

In fact, that's what she had envisioned all those years ago when she started out in med school. She had dreamed of having a small family practice, where she knew everyone's name and could take the time to see patients as she wanted.

She had no illusions though. She wouldn't make the kind of money she was making now or could have made if she had gone into a more lucrative specialty.

But money wasn't the reason she became a doctor. Although, she had years of med school bills to pay.

"Lucas. Do not hit your sister," her mom called, not bothering to take the phone down from her mouth, which made Terry wince from the volume.

She kept the phone to her ear and threw more clothes in her suitcase. She didn't have much in her apartment. She hadn't taken the money to furnish it, since she had been paying down her med school bills as quickly as she could.

The little bit she had bought, she was going to leave. The new tenants could take it or leave it. She was not attached to any of it.

"Let me know how your search goes, okay?" her mom said, sounding harried.

"I will, and you let me know how things go with Sally?" She said a silent prayer for her sister-in-law like she did every time she thought about her.

It didn't look good. She'd already gone through one round of chemo for breast cancer, but it had been in her lymph nodes when they caught it, and now, from what Terry understood, scans had shown it had gone to her bones.

In her experience, and from what she had learned in med school and residency, it was just a matter of time now.

But Sally was a fighter, and she had three children and a really great husband to live for. Terry knew that sometimes God's plans were different than man's plans, and no matter how hard a person fought, and how badly they wanted to stay here on earth, sometimes it was just time.

She swallowed, not liking to think about it and feeling worse than she could imagine for her brother Gilbert. How hard it must be to struggle to figure out what to say to your kids, and still support your wife, and try to earn a living. They'd sold their house and moved in with their mom, who had volunteered to watch the kids and who hadn't minded having some extra bodies in the big old house, since her husband had recently passed.

Which was another thing Terry didn't want to think about. Her dad had made it to her college graduation, but he hadn't seen her become a doctor.

She knew he would have been proud of her, but...

"All right, Mom. I'll not keep you anymore. I'll see you tomorrow, probably late, or maybe the next day. Definitely in church on Sunday."

It was Thursday. She had two days to find housing, Sunday to get prepared, and the doors to her clinic opened on Monday.

It was turnkey, and she was counting on everything running smoothly. Although, she was already expecting that some patients would want to know where Dr. Vivik was and would not like the switcheroo that had happened.

There wasn't anything she could do about that, and she knew she could lose patients.

"Take care, honey," her mom said, sounding tired.

"I love you."

"I love you too, sweetie." Her mom paused. "And I'm really glad you're coming home."

They hung up shortly after, but Terry couldn't deny the fact that her mom was thrilled to have all six of her children back home in Mistletoe Meadows.

Of course, the fact that she'd only been able to get two of them married, and of those two, one was losing his wife, which couldn't sit very well. She wasn't expecting to have kids who went through life single.

Of course, she probably wasn't expecting to lose her husband so early either. They hadn't gotten a chance to enjoy their empty nest. Not that it was empty anymore.

Terry put her hands on her hips and looked around her studio apartment. A small bed, a small kitchen, and a sofa. That was pretty much it, along with a closet and a bathroom.

She hadn't needed much. Hadn't wanted much. Knew this was just a short stop on the way to what she really wanted. She just hadn't expected what she really wanted to come so soon.

Turning around, she took the entire apartment in. The best thing about it was the huge windows that looked out over the cornfields and the horse pasture that edged the town of Richmond. Farmland lay all around it, which was nice. It reminded her of home, although she missed the mountains.

She'd be happy to be back in the Blue Ridge. There was just something that felt protective and cozy about the mountains. Classmates had told her they felt claustrophobic in them, and she supposed if she'd been brought up on the Great Plains, she would have too. But to her, they meant home, and she was more than ready to be home. Especially since the holidays were just around the corner.

Chapter Two

*T*erry couldn't stop the swelling of her heart as she saw the familiar buildings of her hometown. Driving down Main Street was like driving down memory lane. And she smiled as she saw the coffee shop and the courthouse and the road where she would turn to go to her clinic.

But there were no for rent signs anywhere. She'd taken a couple of side streets and looked at different apartment buildings, willing to live anywhere.

She had five siblings, and while one brother had moved back in with her parents, it was possible that one of them might put her up or at least let her stay on the couch.

She hadn't realized that housing was so tight.

The first place she was going to go was her sister Amy's. She had a pet sanctuary outside of town, and while she probably didn't have any room in her one-bedroom bungalow, Amy was often in touch with people, just because of folks stepping out to adopt a pet or drop one off or donate supplies. People sometimes had to give their pets up when they moved, and Amy might know of any places that were available.

She was the only person Terry could think of, but maybe she was panicking just a little. She hadn't realized it was going to be this hard.

Still, it felt good to be back in town, and she smiled as she drove through and out the other side. Farmlands almost immediately opened up on either side of the road, with the mountains rising all around them. Mistletoe Meadows was almost on top of Mistletoe Mountain. And perfectly situated for its name, since they got snow when the lower lying areas didn't.

Still, the views were gorgeous, and she took a moment to admire them. She didn't see views like this in Richmond. Ever.

Her sister didn't live far out of town, and she soon saw the mailbox in the shape of a dog and grinned. It was looking a little ragged, a little older, a little faded, but still beloved and familiar.

Putting her turn signal on, even though there weren't any cars on the road, she pulled down the lane and drove the short distance to Amy's spread.

The familiar bark of dogs greeted her, some of them quite insistent and loud. It sounded like she had a couple of hounds, and there were two large draft horses in the small pasture area.

She didn't often have big animals in her sanctuary, but every once in a while, she got some in.

Those looked well taken care of, and if Terry remembered correctly, they were Percherons.

Amy, carrying a bucket in each hand, walked from the small supply shed to the larger kennel area and looked up. Her eyes narrowed for a moment before her face broke into a big grin. She set the buckets down and came over to Terry's car as she parked it.

"I knew you were coming in today, but I wasn't sure I was going to get to see you!" Amy said as Terry got out and they embraced.

"I can't begin to tell you how good it feels to be home and know that I'm going to get to stay."

"I know you'd always talked about that. It's kind of like your dreams are coming true." Amy lifted her shoulder. "Like getting your doctoral degree wasn't a dream come true."

"Honestly, it's nothing compared to what I feel today. I mean, that was kind of a means to the end, but my goal had always been to come back to my hometown and set up a practice. I can hardly practice without the degree, but this is the completion. The full circle."

"Monday will be the day," Amy said with a knowing smile.

"Exactly," Terry replied, loving that Amy knew exactly how she felt. Monday was the day she would open her clinic, and that would be the day her actual dreams came true.

She looked around, the sky big and open, mountains visible in the distance, and the air feeling fresh and clean. There was just something about mountain air that felt different than air in the low country. Scientifically, she could recite the composition of the air and explain what made it different, but she knew it wasn't just the composition. It was the state of mind that being in the mountains gave her.

"So, are you moving in with Mom like you planned?"

"I don't think so. I might not have a choice. But with Gilbert and everything..." Her voice trailed off, and Amy's expression dropped.

"That's terrible. So sad to think that something like that is happening to such a wonderful person, first of all, and also to such a wonderful family. Honestly, I've struggled sometimes with why God allows that."

"Me too. I'm not going to lie. I've seen a lot of things that just don't seem fair or right, but it's not my responsibility to decide what's fair and right. I'm not God, and I'm not going to pretend to be."

"Well, at least you've retained a little bit of your humility despite your years in med school," Amy teased.

"I think I'm a lot more humble than that," Terry said, laughing. "Although, maybe the fact that I think I am actually shows I'm not."

They laughed together.

"So what are you going to do?" Amy finally said, turning and starting to walk toward where she set the buckets. Terry fell into step with her. She'd helped Amy so often over the last few years, and before that, growing up, they'd always been close. Amy was like her best friend, and now, she was actually going to get to live in the same town.

"I was hoping that you might know someplace that's open. I've searched the ads and looked everywhere, and I just can't find anything."

She had been through a lot in med school and residency. Faced emergencies, seen people die, watched families grieve. She knew, on a scale of importance, whether or not she could find a house was very, very low. At least for her. The pain and suffering that she'd had no idea of before she left for med school had shocked her and had changed her in a lot of different ways. She was a lot more aware of the fact that people were more important than things. That life was transient, not that she hadn't known it before, but it had been brought home to her on multiple levels.

It had made her a better person, she thought. A better Christian too. Everything that she'd been brought up to believe had been borne out in her studies, even though most of the people around her, sometimes it felt like all, were not Christian. They did not believe and would walk away from her because of her beliefs if they knew.

Maybe that's why more people didn't speak out, which was sad. That being an adult, getting a doctorate degree, made her feel like she was back in preschool, where children didn't know any better than to make fun of people they didn't agree with or who were different. But in today's society, it felt like Christians were fair game for otherwise totally sane adults to revert to their childhood and be unkind.

Her sister had picked up her buckets, and she had gone ahead, opening the door where she knew she would be going to put dog food into the feeders.

"Well, I honestly can't think of a single thing. Nothing like what you'd want."

"What was that supposed to mean?"

"You're a doctor now. You probably want something really nice or at least in the nice section of town."

"There aren't very many not-good sections of Mistletoe Meadows. It's not like it's a big town."

"Well, you know what I mean."

She kind of did, although she wouldn't have said there was a bad section anywhere in Mistletoe Meadows. There were just some smaller houses, apartments, and she'd already looked in all of those.

Amy set the buckets down, and though the roar of barking was almost deafening, she stopped at the first pen and petted the muzzle of the dog who stood there.

All of the dogs had outside runs, and Amy cleaned them all every day.

"How's funding?" Terry asked suddenly, knowing that it had always been a struggle for Amy to make enough money to survive and also to feed the animals. Then, she'd gotten a sponsor from a place down the mountain, and she hadn't had to worry about it for several years.

"Funny you should ask," Amy said while measuring out dog food and pouring it into the feeder. "We lost it."

"You lost it?"

"Yeah. Not because of anything we did, but I was training someone to open up another pet sanctuary down closer to the garage that had sponsored us. They shifted their sponsorship from me to them."

"You're kidding!" Terry said, trying not to be outraged. "You mean you actually trained the person who took your funding?"

"I knew when I was doing it that was probably what was going to happen, and in fact I spoke with the Richmond Rebels garage, and they asked me specifically if that was okay. Of course it was okay. I mean, it meant more pets will be able to be saved. I wasn't going to say no."

"What about your funding?"

"I'll just do what I did before. I'll have to have more fundraisers, more eyes in town, make more people aware that they need to donate. I was able to make it before."

"But you expanded on the basis of the funding that you received. You have a lot bigger budget now than you used to."

"Something will happen," Amy said with a smile as she patted the next dog on the head and then poured his food into the bowl. "Maybe I'll have a sister, who happens to be a doctor, because doctors make a lot of money, and maybe she'll open an office in town, and who knows, maybe she'll feel inspired to donate to the cause."

"You know I don't have anything. I've spent everything that I've made since I started working on trying to pay my debts back. You can't imagine what having that kind of debt hanging over the top of your head does to your psyche. I can't stand the stress." She shivered. It was true. She had used a lot of positive thinking techniques, and redirection, to try to keep herself from dwelling on it, but she couldn't stop paying it back with everything she had. She even thought about getting a second job, just so she could pay it back faster. Had anyone ever heard of a doctor with two jobs?

But she admired Amy's faith. She shared it, but it was a faith that said she had to put her boots on and work for it too. She couldn't just pray and assume that God was going to drop it in her lap. That was seldom the way it happened.

It reminded her of her other problem. She was going to need to do something to solve her housing crisis. God wasn't going to just drop a house or apartment in her lap. But He could open something up for her.

"You know, depending on how much you want to fix things up, that old house at the edge of town is for sale."

"The one that they used to give haunted house tours at Halloween?"

She had never gone. She wasn't the slightest bit interested in seeing any kind of haunted house or dealing with the spirit world. God clearly said necromancers were an abomination, and there was no way she was doing anything like that.

Not to mention, she was a scaredy-cat, and it gave her the heebie-jeebies.

"Yeah. That one. It's not very expensive."

"I don't have any money for a down payment. Seriously. Just what is in my bank account from the last two paychecks. Since I write a check out at the beginning of every month toward my student loans." That was after she paid her rent and utilities. She didn't even have a car payment, since she drove around in the one that her dad had helped her buy when she was still in high school.

Thoughts of her dad made her smile, although it made the familiar sad feeling clench around her heart. She missed him.

"Good to know." Amy had moved on to the next dog, petted its head, and fed it. She straightened, putting her hands on her hips and looking up at the ceiling.

"This will be a long shot, but I know that Judd Landis is living in a duplex in town. He's only living on one side from what I can see. And the only reason I know this is because I was out catching a stray cat on that street. Anyway, it looks like the other side is open, although I can't say for sure."

Amy shrugged her shoulders and lifted her hands up. "Maybe someone's living there and they were gone for the day. But I was there for several hours, and I didn't see anyone. The windows look dark too, if you know what I mean. It was early evening by the time I left, and everyone was inside."

It cooled down quickly in the mountains once the sun went down, especially this time of year. They were always ten or more degrees cooler than folks in the valley.

"I see. So he doesn't have an ad up or anything?" Judd Landis was a name she recognized. She thought she went to school with him, but the name didn't really bring a picture to her mind, other than dark hair. And dark eyes.

It wasn't someone she talked to a lot in school. Still, he would be a local boy and would probably know her. Considering that she was one of the most celebrated academic students in the school at the time.

"No. Not that I know of. But I'm not scouring the ads, and I assume you didn't find one."

"No. I didn't," she said, feeling a little foolish as she carried the bucket down to the next pen and used the hose to fill up the water. In the pen was a sweet little terrier mix, very happy and also adorably cute.

"This one's a little darling," she said, bending down and putting her hands in for him to sniff before she started to scratch his head.

"He's sweet, and he breaks my heart a little, because his owner adored him. But her children moved her to a nursing home, and none of her kids wanted her dog. So he came here. He's been here about six months or so."

"That's sad." She scratched his head a little more.

"You can adopt him. You know, I'll even waive the fee for you."

"Wow. Family discount," she said, knowing that her sister worked on donations exclusively and didn't charge anyone anything.

She had a little bit of an in, because her best friend was a veterinarian, and he donated all the spay and neuter operations, as well as the shots to get the animals up to date. It was his contribution to the sanctuary. He also came out and helped. He must have already been at his practice today, since there weren't too many times that she saw Amy without Jones, unless Jones was working.

Chapter Three

"It's hard to believe that we're all grown up," Terry said, remembering how Amy and Jones used to be inseparable when they were younger. In fact, Jones, being an only child, had hung around their family and even gone on several vacations with them.

His family was well-off and he'd had good parents, but he'd been lonely. And he and Amy had bonded better than any friends Terry knew. In fact, if Amy had to choose her best friend, Terry was fairly certain that Jones would beat Terry out along with their other sister.

"I know. Time changes things. But I've been trying to focus on the fact that I can count on it changing. You know? Because...the town is different when we lose people. And like with Teddy there," she pointed to the terrier, "I see it. Not a lot. It's not like every day someone dies and I get their pet, but I get a bunch of them every year. And...it makes me wonder about me. What will happen to my pets when I die?"

"Or get sent to a nursing home by your children," Terry said, somehow thinking that comment would lighten the heavy atmosphere that had descended between them.

She moved down to the next pen and turned the water on.

"No. I don't want to go to a nursing home. I'd rather just die in my shoes. Wherever I'm at."

"Sometimes you don't get a choice. Sometimes your kids grow up and think they know better."

"So far, I don't have any kids, so that's not a problem I'm going to worry about today."

"Probably smart on your part, although I think about it sometimes. It is kinda silly for me to be concerned about it when I don't have children and have no hopes for any."

She tried not to make that sound sad. She had known when she had decided to pursue the career path that she had, that it was going to mean that she was going to miss out on things.

Other people had gotten married in med school or residency, although she had no idea how they had the time to date, let alone plan a wedding. She had been exhausted the entire time. She had barely survived. At least it felt that way.

Regardless, she knew that doing what she had would mean that she wouldn't do the same things everyone else did. And that could include getting married and having children.

"But you're back in your hometown, and you might run into someone. Never say never."

"A positive pep talk from someone who's in basically the same state." Only Amy was younger, so maybe she wasn't quite as... desperate? Sad? Terry wasn't quite sure how to describe herself.

"Well, here's another pep talk," Amy said as she scratched the head of the poodle mix. "Go to Judd, ask if you can rent the duplex, and even if he says no, find out if it's empty. Ask him why not. You can do this."

"That was a pep talk?" Terry asked, narrowing her eyes and feeling like she missed the point.

"Sure. I'm just saying, he's your last hope, throw yourself at his feet and beg for his mercy." She shrugged, dumping food into the next bowl.

"Maybe I'll just see if you have any empty pens."

"Actually, I don't. I have two dogs in the house with me right now because I didn't have a place for them."

"Wow," Terry said, her brows coming down. "You've never been that full. You just expanded last year."

"I know. I probably need to get out and talk about adoption a little more. Taking care of all these animals is almost a full-time job. I still need to clean the pens after I'm done with this, and that's just the dogs."

"Yeah. I saw you had horses out there."

"I'm actually renting the space for those. Someone approached me and asked if I would. It's not much, but it's a little bit of income."

"You take care of them?" Terry asked, knowing that was something that Amy had never done while she had been helping her. But whatever worked, whatever brought them money, and Amy would never turn down an animal.

"Yes. I had never been around horses too much, but it turns out I like them. Who knew?"

"They're big," Terry said as they made it down the first row and walked around the end. There was a row of pens and runs along the back.

"But they're so gentle. They're sweet. And I see them in town when the person uses them. People love them."

"Who is it?" Terry asked, knowing that she probably knew the person.

"They asked me not to say." Amy said, and while she gave an apologetic look, she didn't sound scared or concerned that Terry might be upset. After all, she probably figured that Terry was an adult and could understand if someone wanted to keep their privacy.

"Got it," she said.

Amy grinned. "You'll see them sometime, most likely. Typically on weekends, they're out. And it's a great tourist attraction."

"I bet so. If they're pulling a wagon with them, that would be something a lot of people would like to do."

"It is. And that's the thing with Mistletoe Meadows. We need the tourist industry to survive, since we don't have any industry of our own. So many people make their living off of that." She lifted her brows as she stood in front of the first pen, petting a lab mix, who stood still for about two seconds before it was bouncing off the walls. "And you will be too. I mean, I know it's not direct, but the people that you treat make their living off the tourist industry. If that goes south, they'll have to move, and eventually you will too."

"Not if I keep my expenses down. As long as I don't have a whole lot of overhead, I don't have to make a lot to pay my bills. And that's the beauty of having my student loans paid off. Although, I wish I would cut back a bit, because I'd really love to be able to donate to you right now. This is crazy. Don't you ever feel stress over this?"

She would be reeling under the stress of having animals to take care of and wondering where their next meal was going to come from.

"Every night, I put it in God's hands. And every morning, I try not to pick it back up. Eventually, by the end of the day, I figure out that I'm carrying it again, and so I go to the Lord again and tell Him that I'm willing to take care of His creatures, but He's going to have to provide funds. Although, I know I'm going to have to do some of the legwork to get those funds."

Amy had such a great faith. Terry had always admired it, and maybe that was one of the reasons why they were such great friends. Or maybe that was one of the reasons why she considered Amy such a great friend.

She hoped that she was a friend like that, although she felt like she had a lot of growing to do before she hit that type of spirituality.

"All right. Thanks for your expertise. I'll text you later. Although, if things don't work out with Judd, I might be forced to stay at Mom's. As much as I hate to."

"Don't say it like that. Sally might feel better having a doctor in the house."

"From what I heard, she's not there much. Neither is Gilbert."

"True. That's what I've seen too, but I haven't talked to Mom about it a whole lot. I think when she sees me, she wants to get her mind off of it."

"Maybe they'd like to adopt the dog."

"She already has, and Gilbert just rolled his eyes and shook his head whenever I asked. I assumed it wasn't a good time to extol the virtues of how children should grow up with dogs, and every child should have man's best friend."

"All right. Wish me luck."

"I'll pray that God gives you what you need."

Terry chuckled and threw up a hand as she walked around the corner and back down the long walkway, into the sunshine.

Judd might say yes, or he might say no. She wouldn't know until she asked. And as much as she wasn't sure she wanted to live in a duplex, especially beside a man she didn't really know, she figured that would be better than living with her mom right now.

She should have asked Amy more about Judd.

She'd remember to do that next time, she was sure.

Chapter Four

She checked the address that Amy had given her again.

Yep, this dark, brooding house, with only one front door, was the duplex Amy told her about.

When Terry thought about duplexes, she thought about two separate front doors and a house that was entirely split down the middle, with one family on one side and one family on the other.

How was that possible with only one front door?

She couldn't resist sending a text to her sister.

> Are you sure this is the right address?

The reply came back quickly.

> Yep. I know it doesn't look like a duplex, but it is.

> Okay, thanks.

She sighed as she texted back.

She wasn't nervous exactly. She'd been through a lot worse in med school. She chuckled to herself, thinking not for the first time that that might have been one of the purposes of med school, to give her something to compare every terrible thing that ever happened in her life to. Like, if she could survive med school, she could survive anything.

Taking a breath, she yanked the latch of her car, gave it an extra hard shove, because it stuck sometimes, and got out.

She hadn't even thought to ask her sister if Judd would be home. Or what he did for a living.

Maybe he was working.

> Does Judd have a job?

She needed to stop texting her sister.

> He's a landscaper in the summer, does odd jobs in the winter, and snow removal of course. He also does maintenance work for different places, including the church, and he probably even has helped Dr. Vivik at times. You may want to talk to him about that while you're there.

It took a while for Amy to write that text out, and her phone buzzed as she was standing in front of the one front door.

She rapped, not seeing a doorbell, and hoping once more that she wasn't making a huge mistake. Maybe she should have moved in with her mother.

After shuffling from one foot to the other and feeling like several minutes had gone by, she rapped on the door again. Maybe he was in the bathroom. Maybe he didn't answer the door for strangers. Maybe he was working.

Okay, Lord, if he doesn't answer on the third knock, I'm going to go to Mom's. Maybe that's where You want me anyway. Maybe I'm supposed to be helping with Sally, like Amy suggested.

Although, she might have "doctor" in front of her name, that didn't mean that she was going to be any better at taking care of someone who was dying of cancer than anyone else could. Typically a person's loved ones took care of them better than anyone else. Unless they had been doing it for a long time and were weary. Weariness had a tendency to cause a person to make mistakes.

Lifting her hand, deciding that maybe she hadn't been knocking loud enough, she decided she would really smack on the door, and that was how she ended up punching Judd Landis in the face the first time she met him.

Chapter Five

*J*udd blinked, feeling pain shoot through his head, down his elbows, and almost immediately his entire face felt like it was three times bigger than its usual size.

The lady in front of him didn't look like she meant to hit him. She didn't look like a threat; in fact, she looked like...Terry McBride.

Amy had mentioned she might be coming.

He had been out until almost three AM the night before cleaning the courthouse building. He cleaned it at night so he didn't get in the way of their using it during the day. On the weekends, it was locked up tight. He could get in, but that gave him the weekends for his other jobs.

Regardless, he had just gotten up.

And now he felt like he was missing something.

She didn't look like she was pulling her fist back for a second punch, and instead, she was talking.

"I'm so sorry! I was going to knock again. I've already knocked twice, and I just wanted to make sure you heard it, so I was going to knock as hard as I could and wasn't expecting you to open the door really fast."

"Because you already knocked twice." That was why he had opened the door fast. He didn't mention that he had been expecting her or was at least looking for her. Or he might have stayed in bed another hour.

"Right, and you were trying to get there before I left." She shook her head, and she looked so abashed and regretful that he almost smiled. He tried to make it a point not to smile too much. He was of the mind that scarcity made smiles more meaningful.

Or at least that's what his mom always teased him about. He just was not a natural smiler. He kinda had to think about it before his face moved.

He didn't know anyone else with that problem, so maybe it was just him, or maybe he'd end up reading a book someday and finding out that half the world was like him, and he'd grown up without knowing it.

Regardless, he looked at the woman standing in front of him, already knowing what she was probably going to ask and knowing what he was going to say.

Amy was good. He had to give her that.

"So, I'm going to have a bit of a weird request, but you might know my sister Amy McBride."

"Amy? McBride?" He scrunched up his nose, pretending to think.

"Yeah. She's...my sister. And she also runs the pet sanctuary up on the hill."

"There's a pet sanctuary?"

He was terrible at this. Really awful, but Amy had asked him to pretend to be surprised. Or confused, acting like he didn't know what she was talking about.

Typically, Judd didn't really have to spend a whole lot of time pretending. What most people said went right over his head. He just thought about things, noticed things, but didn't really talk about them.

"Yes. Well, never mind. If you don't know about it, it's not going to help. Anyway, I heard you might be willing to rent out your duplex."

He drew his brows down, and then, as though he didn't quite understand what she was saying, he stuck his thumb in his belt and looked left and then right. Then, he straightened back up, looked her in the eye, and said, "Does this look like a duplex?"

That took the wind out of her sails. He could see her deflate, bite her lip, and look off to the side as she said, "No?"

He almost asked, "what makes you think it is," but he bit his tongue and just stayed silent.

"Amy said it was," she said in a small voice, which tugged on his heartstrings, more than he wanted to admit.

"I see."

He didn't say anything else, like, "it actually is a duplex, it just doesn't look like it from the outside," which was why he was questioning her, except that wasn't entirely true. He was questioning her because Amy asked him to play dumb.

There were a lot of people who would joke and say that it wasn't hard for him to play dumb. At least, he assumed they would be joking.

"So is it?" she finally asked, when he said nothing else. He'd found that if he stayed quiet, people had a tendency to talk. He just had to be able to live through the awkward moments until they finally figured out that he wasn't going to say anything, so they had to.

"Yes," he answered.

"So... Are both sides rented out?"

"No."

Her eyes slid sideways again, which was something she seemed to do when she was thinking. Interesting.

"Are you interested in renting it out?"

He pretended to think about it. After all, this was supposed to be a surprise. He didn't have it advertised anywhere, and he really wasn't interested in renting it out. Except to Terry.

"I might be."

"If?"

"Depends on who, I guess," he said easily, like he hadn't taken the hint that she was interested.

He leaned against the doorframe, the pain in his face dulling to a mild thump. He was pretty sure he was going to have a black eye. That might be an interesting story to tell, if he told stories.

"What about me?"

"Do we know each other?" He tilted his head, like he was studying her, trying to figure out if he missed something.

"I think we went to school together."

He almost laughed. They had gone to school together. They'd graduated together too. But while he knew all about her, he was pretty sure she didn't have a clue about him. Despite the fact that they'd spent six years in homeroom together. Since her name started with an M, and his with an L. They'd not sat side by side, but close.

He probably should be offended over that, but he went out of his way to make himself...not invisible, just not draw attention to himself. His parents hadn't cared, but his grandmother had drilled that into his head. *Let your actions speak for you. You don't need to have people looking at you, getting attention for what you're doing. Let them see Jesus in you.*

He heard that all of his life growing up, and it meshed with his naturally reticent personality. He was never one of the people who enjoyed getting up and having all eyes on him. He was much more comfortable in the back of the class. He might have cracked jokes, except while he enjoyed making people laugh, he didn't really enjoy the attention that came with being the one who'd made the joke.

"What year did you graduate?" he finally asked, since she seemed to be trying to figure out what to say, and she could hardly say, "I don't really remember you."

Although he supposed she could. It just wouldn't be conducive to convincing him to rent out the apartment. She had no idea that he had every intention of renting the apartment to her, and had, in fact, spent the day yesterday cleaning it up.

She named the year, and he pretended to look surprised. "Yeah. We graduated the same year. Funny that."

"I thought so. I mean, your name sounded familiar when Amy said it, but I couldn't really put a face to it. But the dark eyes and dark hair were kind of what I pictured in my head. Only, I kinda pictured you without a black eye."

He almost lost it there. He was pretty sure she was making a joke.

"If you'd have seen me before you knocked on the door, you might have recognized me."

She snorted and laughed. "I really am sorry about that."

"Hey, it could happen to anyone. I mean, it's never happened to me, but that's not saying it couldn't."

"Yeah. Stop trying to make me feel better. You're just...going overboard there."

He liked it. She wasn't letting him intimidate her. Sometimes his silences could be disconcerting, and she was plowing through. Of course, she was desperate to have a place to live too.

"Do you think that you might be able to rent me your empty duplex?"

"How much noise are you planning on making?" he asked, barely able to keep a straight face.

"Oh, I'm very quiet."

"Do you have pets?"

"No..." She drew the word out, and he drew his brows down right away.

"I don't have a no pet policy, but only because I've never rented out that side before."

"I don't have any pets. I kind of wanted one, since I love animals, but I couldn't have one in the city."

"I see. So you think country people are...dirtier?"

That was not a fair question, and he almost didn't ask it, and he probably should stop messing with her. Amy had asked him to play dumb, not scare her away. And he wasn't sure how determined she was to rent from him.

Still, he hadn't given in easy, and he was pretty sure she had no idea he'd been waiting on her. That had been the goal.

"Of course I don't."

"It kinda sounded that way."

"No. I just meant, where I lived before, they didn't allow me to have pets. I wanted one. And now that I'm finally back here in Mistletoe Meadows, I was kinda thinking that I could, especially since I just visited Amy—"

"Her pet sanctuary, or something?"

"Yeah. And she has a terrier mix. It's just adorable."

"Everyone adopts golden retrievers."

"You're probably right. You're not really worried about them biting you, or attacking your family, the way you might a different dog, like a German shepherd, or a rottweiler, or a pit bull."

He jerked his chin and didn't say anything.

"Anyway. If you don't allow pets, that's fine. I just...didn't mean anything by it."

"You can have pets." He held up a hand. "No goats in the house."

He was pretty sure she was swallowing a laugh or a snort or something. She looked a little bit like her cheeks puffed out, and then her neck stretched out, and then she nodded slowly, her face completely serious. "I won't bring any goats in the house."

"All right. There might be more rules, but that's number one."

"Got it." She swallowed, looked at the ground for a moment, and then back up. "Does this mean I have it?"

"Means I'm thinking about it. Don't you want to see it first?"

"Okay."

He pushed away from the doorjamb. "You're going to come in the house, and you're not gonna punch me in the face again. Okay?"

"We did get off to a bad start. I really am sorry about that."

"I just wanted to lay some ground rules down."

"Got it. No punching. No goats."

"Well. I think you're smart. I kinda remember you being on the positive side of average."

"Yeah. I have, sometimes, been told that I'm rather intelligent."

He kept his face serious. It was hilarious that she hadn't told him that she was a doctor. He wondered why she hadn't. He couldn't believe that she missed the opportunity to put him in his place.

Or maybe she was still trying to figure out why he felt like he needed to tell her that there were no goats allowed in the house.

The look on her face was priceless. He almost wished he had a camera. Amy would get a huge kick out of this.

Chapter Six

Jerry stepped inside, wondering what in the world she'd gotten herself into. The man seemed...nuts.

Of course, he was still entertaining the idea of renting to her, after she poked him in the face. So, she supposed he had every right to be a little bit strange, but...she'd never met anyone so...different.

She wasn't getting any bad vibes from him though. Not that she totally trusted her sense of intuition, but she did rely on it to give her a feel for what was going on. She'd even learned in med school that a person's subconscious picked up things that their conscious brain might not. So, even if a doctor couldn't see anything, if they're thinking that there might be a problem, more tests might be a good idea.

It wasn't exactly something they had been tested on, but she'd seen it happen over and over.

He closed the door behind them, and she looked around where they stood. It was a shared foyer with steps that led upstairs.

"I live on this side." He pointed to a door on the right, right at the bottom of the steps, then indicated one on the left. "That would be yours. You'll have to get a key made for the lock. I don't have one."

"There is no lock?" she said, unable to keep the incredulity out of her voice, before she remembered that it was Mistletoe Meadows. And she probably sounded ridiculous. She bet half the population didn't lock their doors.

"There's nothing over there. The outside door has a lock, but I'll have to find the key. And you might have to get a duplicate made since I don't have extras."

"All right. If you're going to lock it, I'll get a key made."

"We can leave it open. It's up to you." He shrugged his shoulders. He was acting a little bit more normal now, although he still didn't seem like the most talkative person. Maybe that's why she didn't really remember him. Even though they must have been in homeroom together, if they graduated the same year. But for the life of her, she couldn't remember. She spent most of her homeroom studying. It wasn't that she didn't have friends or never talked to anyone, but she was trying to get the best grades she could.

"The kitchen's at the end of the hall." He pointed down the hall, past where her door was.

"So... We share a kitchen?" she asked as he pointed to the opening at the end of the hall. She could see a table with a couple of chairs, and a counter beside the sink, and a window. The window faced the back lot, which had a gorgeous view of the mountains she could see from here.

The view pulled at her heart, and she almost started forward. She could stand at the sink and look out at the mountains. That wouldn't be a hardship.

"Aren't you going to look at it?" He indicated the door to her left.

She didn't say anything but turned to the left, opening the door. It creaked open, although it wasn't dusty, like she would have expected.

The room inside was completely bare, big windows that faced the street and windows on the side. A fireplace at the far end. She could imagine cozy winter nights with a cheerful fire crackling in the fireplace, while she sat in a chair cozied up and reading, or just relaxing after a long day at work, and petting her dog, not goat.

What had that been about? Had he been serious?

She shook her head.

"Nice big room," she said. It would be chilly away from the fireplace, unless the heat was on, but there was plenty of room for bookshelves and another chair or two.

She pointed at the door at the end. "Does that go into the kitchen?"

"No. It's an office."

She glanced at him, and when he didn't move, she walked into the room, looking around, appreciating the high ceiling and the chandelier that hung from it.

That was a little dusty, which didn't make sense. Why would it be dusty when the floor wasn't?

Odd.

But she kept walking, curious about this office.

As she opened the door, she realized that it must have been built off of the kitchen, since there were huge floor-to-ceiling windows that gave the same view that she had just seen over the sink. The mountains in the distance, with the rolling hills in the foreground and foothills off to the left. There wouldn't be much room for bookshelves in this room, since two of the walls were mostly windows. But she loved it.

"This is nice," she said. She supposed she'd find out if she actually needed an office or not. Probably to do payroll or at least figure it out. But the receptionist would process insurance claims, according to Dr. Vivik, and she hopefully wouldn't have a huge number of things to do at home.

"There is no way to get in the kitchen from this room," she said, although she assumed he already knew it.

"No."

She didn't like that. If it were her house, she would put a doorway from the living room into the kitchen.

She walked back to where he still stood at the entrance to the living room.

"I'd like to see the kitchen," she said, and he jerked his head, waiting for her to go through, and if she wasn't mistaken, there was a bit of humor in his eyes as she walked past. Maybe thinking about her punching him when he had opened the door, and he was staying out of the reach of her fists.

"I really didn't mean to," she said as she started down the hall.

He laughed, and that's when she knew she was right on about what he had been thinking.

The kitchen was huge. With a big table that seated six or could easily do eight with more chairs. It seemed a little newer than the rest of the house.

"And we would share this? Are there rules for the kitchen?"

He opened his mouth.

She cut him off. "Other than no goats."

"That's rule number one. Always. For every room in the house," he said, like he was teaching her something.

"Thanks. That really is going to be a hardship for me, but...I'll follow your rules. If you insist."

"I fear I must," he said. His eyes twinkled again.

She noticed his lips didn't seem to move up much, but she could tell that he was smiling because of the twinkle in his eyes.

She hadn't read about any conditions like that, where a person couldn't smile, but she also wasn't so naïve as to think that she actually had learned about every condition that was known to man. Of course, he might not have a condition at all. It might just be the way he was.

"This is lovely."

"I don't have much in the fridge," he said, and she assumed that that meant she could put anything wherever she wanted to.

"I probably won't either." Cooking for one didn't require a lot of groceries. She'd gotten okay at it over the years. At different times, she'd shared houses and apartments with roommates, but almost always, they cooked for themselves and didn't have a cooking or cleaning schedule. Each person was just responsible for themselves.

She still was trying to get over her surprise that it was an actual duplex. Did she want to share a kitchen with this man?

"Bedrooms are upstairs," he said in a monotone, and she followed him back out of the kitchen. Knowing very well that the bedrooms were upstairs, but wanting to see them. Although, did it matter? Seriously? Was she going to say no to this and move in with her mom and her brother and his wife and their three kids and descend into the whole cancer thing?

She didn't think so. Right now, her brother needed their mom's full attention, and their mom didn't need to be worried about her.

She climbed the stairs first, and he followed. The banister was beautifully carved and seemed old, along with the rest of the house, which had wood floors that seemed like maybe they had been recently sanded but not stained.

As she got to the top, she saw a bathroom right beside her and a hall with two doors on the left and one door on the right.

"My bedroom's on that side. It takes up the whole side of the house." He pointed to the two doors on the other side. "There used to be two bedrooms, but someone took the dividing wall out, and now it's just one room."

"It must be huge," she said. If it took up the entire side of the house, it would be the same length as the living room and the width of the kitchen.

"This side isn't tiny."

Opening the door, she looked, and indeed, the entire room was massive. And it already had a bed. There was just a bare mattress on it, no box springs, but it was a bed. She wasn't going to have to try to find one, figure out how she was going to get it moved, and that was really all the furniture she needed. Although need was relative, since she could have slept on the floor. Would have. Even use an air mattress, rather than spending a lot of money on something that she wasn't sure she would keep. Once things shook out with Gilbert and his wife, she probably would move back in with her mom. Her mom had been by herself after their dad died, and she assumed that she must have been lonely. She had said so multiple times, and every time, it made Terry feel bad that she wasn't able to move back.

Regardless, she wasn't in the market for a house. Not right now.

"The closet's pretty big."

Judd wasn't one to talk a lot. If she were showing the house, she'd probably be talking a mile a minute, telling them every wonderful thing about it, but he really didn't need to say anything. There were huge windows, letting in a lot of light, and the ceiling in the bedroom was just as tall as the one downstairs. She loved the old houses with the high ceilings. There was a large fireplace that probably backed against each wall although she'd have to check the other bedroom to be sure.

She had already started walking to the closet, and he was right, it was a big walk-in closet with its own light.

Not that she had that many clothes. But she wouldn't need to buy a dresser.

"It's perfect. If you'll rent it to me, I'll take it."

She had said that before she was able to ask herself again, was she okay sharing a bathroom?

Because that's what this would mean. A bathroom and a kitchen and an entrance.

"You haven't seen the bathroom yet."

"I don't need to. Unless there are snakes in it, I'm going to take it."

"Hold on a second, I'd better get Bowie out of there."

"Bowie?"

"What I call my boa constrictor. Not very original, I know."

"You said no goats."

"Because goats eat snakes."

"They don't eat boa constrictors." She shouldn't argue with him. He was kidding, and she knew it. And he knew she knew it.

He lifted a brow, but still no smile, as he turned and walked to the door, holding it open until she had walked through and then closing it behind her, that same smirk on his face, in his eyes, if not on his mouth.

She walked to the bathroom, and it was simple. A shower and tub, a sink and toilet. A couple of racks to hang towels on and a closet at the back.

"I'll take it." She took a breath. "If you're willing."

"Maybe we should go over all the rules."

He didn't seem to be kidding. But his first rule was no goats, so he couldn't possibly be serious, right? She never met someone who kept her completely off balance like he had. And yet, she found herself comfortable in his presence. If that was possible. He just...was different than anyone she knew.

"All right."

"I'm not charging rent, and the utilities are together."

"There are no separate utilities?"

"No. So I'll take care of those."

"What will I take care of?" she asked. She couldn't take this place if she didn't pay.

"We'll figure it out. Those are all the rules." He put a hand up. "Take it or leave it."

Just like that? They weren't going to discuss this? "Hold on a second. I can't not pay rent."

"All right. That's fine, if you don't want it. I wasn't really looking for a renter."

"But I'm not a renter if I don't pay rent!" she said, getting a little huffy despite herself. The man was infuriating.

"Okay," he said, walking back down the hall and starting down the steps.

"Hold on!" she said, her voice starting to screech just a little, even though she had no intention of allowing it to do so.

"You said you didn't want it."

"I didn't!" The idea of moving in with her mother and overwhelming her kept her following him down the steps.

"All right. Fine. I agree." She'd just leave cash sitting around somewhere, to pay him at least for the utilities. He couldn't pay for everything; that wasn't fair. She wasn't asking for a handout. She was just asking for a place to stay.

"Fine. I can give you the key, once I find it. If you want to make a duplicate, and if you want to change your lock, that's fine. Otherwise, I'm going to go get some breakfast."

"Breakfast?" She looked at her phone. It was almost eleven.

What in the world did he do? Amy had said that he did odd jobs, but did he really sleep in until eleven? How was he going to survive if she wasn't paying rent and...

"Is this going to get repossessed while we're living here? Do you have a deed? Are you just squatting here?" The idea had just come to her. Maybe she shouldn't have said it, but it slipped out.

That would explain why he didn't have a key, why he wasn't charging rent, and how he was able to afford it when sleeping in until eleven o'clock in the morning.

"No, yes, no."

She had to think back about it and try to figure out what she had asked and in what order to try to figure out what his answers were.

The man was infuriating. No joke.

"All right. Well, I have my stuff in my car. There's not much. But I'll probably go and get some cleaning supplies and some food. Do you need anything?" She almost slapped her hand over her mouth. She wasn't going to become his go-get-stuff girl. Except, he was allowing her to rent for free. She could buy the groceries.

"No. I'm fine. Thanks."

Well, there went that idea. He wasn't going to let her get anything. Which was probably just as well. Maybe she should cook for him, but she wasn't that great of a cook. She could make enough food to keep herself from starving, as long as she didn't mind eating a lot of salad, which she didn't. She'd seen firsthand the effect of obesity and had voluntarily taken as many nutrition classes as they had allowed her to in college.

Well, it had been an interesting hour, but she did have a place to stay. And that had been the goal. She could consider the morning a success.

Chapter Seven

"So she actually rented from you?" Wilson McBride said as he stuck a foot on the shovel and shoved it into the dirt.

Judd nodded. "She did." He slammed his own shovel into the ground. He'd found a kindred spirit in Wilson. Wilson was considered a golden boy, the favorite of the family, and the town favorite as well. It seemed like everything he touched succeeded, and everyone loved him.

But there was more to Wilson than met the eye, and Judd had gotten to know him pretty well over the last few years. They'd done a lot of things together to benefit their town.

"Until she figures out that your house isn't really a duplex?"

Judd laughed. "Nah, I think the rule about the goats got her thinking too hard for her to be able to spend her brainpower on anything else."

"That girl has a lot of brainpower to spare," Wilson said, without any trace of hyperbole.

"I know." Judd knew she was brilliant. That she could have done a lot more than just been a doctor in a family practice. She could have specialized in anything she wanted to do, but despite her intelligence, her goal had always been to come back to Mistletoe Meadows. At least that's what Wilson had said.

Judd just remembered her being smart in school, and honest. She didn't let people cheat off her, like other smart kids did. A backscratching thing often went on.

He shut the thought out of his head. High school was a long time ago, and until he had children of his own, he didn't need to think about it anymore. Other than possibly catching a game on Friday nights.

"You know you're asking for trouble having her there," Wilson said conversationally as he continued to dig a hole for the fence that they were putting in. Amy had needed to expand for a while, and she didn't have the money. So Wilson and he had gotten together to donate the materials and the labor to put in more pens for her.

Amy did not know where the material had come from. They had said it was an anonymous donation. It was something that they did a lot of.

Today was a lot colder, with a brisk wind blowing. The leaves that had already turned golden brown were floating down by the bucket loads over the fields that lined the high meadows.

The mountains in the distance looked less blue green and more blue brown.

Regardless of the season, Judd loved the way the mountains looked. And he'd endure a few colder temperatures to be able to live on top of one. The views were indescribable.

"I know," he said in reply to Wilson's comment as he dumped another shovelful of dirt next to the hole that he was digging.

They were about eight feet apart, although they could see and hear each other easily. Both of them were wearing gloves. It was just that time of year. They would still have some more decent weather before winter really set in.

"I'm just going to have to be careful, that's all."

"We could bring her in. She is the doctor in town. She probably has a few ideas of her own," Wilson said. "Plus, Terry really does have a good heart. Despite all of her intelligence. I know, I grew up with her."

Judd knew that Wilson was just four years younger than Terry and he admired his older sister a lot.

If Judd didn't know better, he'd almost feel like Wilson and Amy were conspiring to push him toward Terry, but that was ridiculous. He'd barely graduated from high school, he was terrible in academics, and he didn't really have a good job. He just...worked wherever he could, wanting to stay in town. He didn't really have anything that he could do to earn money from the tourists, so he did odd handyman jobs and the other things on the side.

But he did know better. So he brushed it aside, just assuming that they were making him part of the family, as they had a tendency to do. After all, it's what they had done with Jones, Amy's best friend.

"Are you gonna be at Sunday dinner?"

He'd resisted going to their Sunday dinners for a long time. It was something the McBride family did, just every Sunday they gathered at their mom's house. Everybody brought something, and they all ate. Anyone who could go went. Terry had been away at med school and residency and hadn't made one for years.

Judd had gone a few times over the years, but he usually declined. Although, Wilson and Amy both had been more insistent lately that he go, and he'd been to three out of the last four.

"If I think of something to take," he said, shoving his shovel down in the dirt. "Why didn't we rent a skid loader and a post hole digger attachment?"

"We'd be done by now, wouldn't we?" Wilson said with a laugh.

Judd knew why they hadn't. They were saving money. It was easier for them to use their manpower and save the hundreds of dollars it would have taken to rent the equipment.

Both of them were old school that way. Plus, he didn't go to the gym, so he needed to do something to beef up his biceps.

He almost laughed out loud at the thought.

They kept working, and his mind drifted to Terry. Although he knew it shouldn't. Now that she was back in town, opening up a family practice, and ready to settle down, she wasn't going to be looking at a guy like him.

There were a couple of law offices by the courthouse and some other professionals in town and scattered around the outskirts.

A couple of nice horse farms set lower on the mountain. He had no idea what those people did for a living.

There were some folks who worked in DC during the week and came out to Mistletoe Meadows on the weekends. Locals didn't care for them too much, because most of the time, their views were vastly different from the folks who lived around there.

Their values were too.

But it was more of a live and let live situation, and whether their values aligned with the locals or not, their money was just as good.

That was probably the kind of husband Terry would get. She'd meet some bigwig from Congress hanging around town, and fall in love, or at least decide that he was good enough to get married to.

"I didn't realize you guys were starting today! I would have come out to help you." Amy came over, sounding a little breathless, with two dogs on leashes running around her.

"That's the reason we didn't tell you," Wilson said, making Judd laugh.

"You guys are incorrigible," Amy said. "I can't give you a hand right now, because as soon as I'm done walking these dogs, Jones has time to do three cats for me. I'm going to run them over."

"That's fine. We weren't planning on you. Although, if you want to throw food, go ahead."

Judd envied the easy rapport that Wilson had with his sister. The whole family seemed to have it, just a respect for each other, and they actually liked each other. Of course, just having siblings would have been nice. But that hadn't been his lot either.

"If you would have told me, I could have made you something. I don't have time now. You can go in and make sandwiches if you want."

"Thanks, sis," Wilson said. Judd knew that neither of them would go in. She barely had enough money to feed herself and buy food for the animals. They certainly weren't going to take food out of her refrigerator.

"Will you have time to finish this up tomorrow?" Wilson asked after Amy walked away. Wilson had a farm he had to take care of, but once he had his animals taken care of for the morning, he didn't need to go back until evening most days, unless he had hay to make or some other farm chores to do. Basically, they worked around Judd's schedule.

"I told Mrs. Blackburn that I'd help her get her old refrigerator out of the house. She has a new one coming, and the store will deliver, but they were going to charge her to take the old one away."

"Gotcha," Wilson said.

They worked in silence for a while, and maybe it was because they had already put in two sides, this was their third, and maybe they were getting better at it. But it didn't take as long as what he was thinking, and definitely one more good day would get them finished.

"That wasn't so bad," Wilson said as he shoveled gravel around the top of the last cement they poured.

All the posts to hold the outside wiring in place were in and cemented.

Judd put the level that he'd been using to keep the post straight in with the rest of his tools.

"Not bad work for a few hours," he said easily. He had things to do, and Wilson would have to get back and take care of his animals.

"I know you're going to go over there and pet those big galoots," Wilson said as Judd finished putting his tools away.

"They have names," he said, knowing that Wilson knew full well they had names. He'd helped him name them.

"I know. As big and scary looking as they are, I can't believe how gentle and easygoing they are."

"That's part of what they're bred for. You can't have a horse that big and have them going crazy on you all the time like a Thoroughbred."

"I think that was a slam."

"Do you own Thoroughbreds?"

"Not yet," Wilson said, and they laughed together. Wilson wasn't exactly a horse lover. He had beef cattle that kept the farm in the black, although barely some years.

They went over to the horses together, and when the horses saw them, they came over to the fence.

Judd pulled out a sugar cube and held it flat on his hand as he reached up to scratch Bob's wide head.

"They sure do look a lot better than the first time we saw them," Wilson said as he scratched Belle, who sniffed him, hoping for a sugar cube.

"Here you go, you big galoot," Judd said as he gave Belle the sugar cube that he'd saved for her.

Sugar wasn't any better for horses than it was for people, so he tried not to go overboard and only gave them one or two treats a day.

"They sure do," Judd said, running a hand down Bob's powerful neck. It was soft and silky, although the winter hair was coming in nicely. He didn't have much of a mane and even less of a tail which had been bobbed. But his old bones had filled in rather nicely, and Wilson and he had agreed that they were ready for some work, which was why they'd started using them to pick the kids up several weeks prior. They had rescued them from the kill pen down in the valley several months ago.

They had wondered for a while why their owner might have gotten rid of them, but it seemed like maybe because of foot trouble. Oftentimes, drafts weren't trained to pick up their feet, and their hooves broke off naturally. The problem was, if they got an infection, it was difficult to treat them, since they weren't used to having their feet handled.

Regardless, they found a good farrier, who had been willing to work with them, although at first, he'd had to sedate them.

He and Wilson had put up some stocks, which were basically things that made it easier for the farrier to work on their feet.

And while the problems hadn't completely gone away, they'd been able to get them the care they needed. Judd had only been kicked once, by Bob, when he'd first started trying to teach him to pick up his back feet.

It had smarted for quite a long time.

If Terry had been in town, maybe he'd have gone down to the clinic, just to make sure he wasn't going to have some blood clot end up in his lungs. Different people had asked him, and he just shrugged. He supposed if it was his time to go, it was his time. Although, he kinda thought that it wasn't going to be from a kick in the thigh.

Regardless, they spent a lot of time and a good bit of money on the horses, but they were hoping that it would pay off as they were expecting to use them for a tourist attraction.

"These poor guys don't know we're about ready to put them to work," Wilson said, and Judd nodded. "They've been doing great with the kids on Sundays. Especially Belle."

"I kinda think Bob's going to let her do the lion's share of it."

"Well, Bob's going to have to pull his share too," Judd said firmly.

He loved both horses equally, but he really did love Belle's willingness and her heart to please her owner.

Horses were a little bit like dogs in that way. He had the feeling that he could ask Belle to do anything, and Belle would do it for him.

It was a heavy responsibility though, because he didn't want to push Belle further than what she could go and end up hurting her. A horse like Bob, that probably wasn't going to happen.

"All right, I'd better get home. I still have a couple hours' worth of work to do."

"Same," Judd said, less about the hours of work and more about needing to get home. He was wondering what Terry had been doing. And was hoping to catch a few winks before he went in to clean the courthouse. He'd gotten the message from his boss that there was a heater panel that was broken, and they also wanted him to look at a window latch that seemed to be sticking.

Why in the world someone would want to be opening a window, he had no idea, but it was just his job to fix them, not try to make sense out of the things that other people did.

And he was happy that he had the work, so he wasn't complaining.

"Don't forget about dinner on Sunday," Wilson said as he smacked him on the back and walked away. "Bring your poppy seed chicken casserole. It was pretty good last time we had it."

He laughed. He'd forgotten about that. He probably could put that together pretty easily, and to his surprise, the first time he made it, he actually really liked it. He hadn't realized that poppy seeds were a thing and that they could end up making chicken casserole taste really good. Different, like he'd made a completely new dish, but still good.

Maybe he'd do that. Although, he wasn't quite sure what Terry was going to think when she saw him there. The idea made him smile. She couldn't be any more surprised than she had been when he'd opened the door and she'd punched him in the face.

Come to think of it, he hadn't even told Wilson the story. Not that he would. He wouldn't want to embarrass Terry. Because Wilson would definitely rub it in.

Chapter Eight

"Thanks for helping me, Tris," Terry said as she stood and looked at the walls in the waiting room.

They'd taped it up and stuck a coat of fresh paint on it, which had made her feel marginally better. Like she was doing something to get ready. It felt like she shouldn't be able to just walk in and make the place hers.

"Anytime," Tris said, standing beside Terry and admiring their handiwork.

Tris had gotten married the previous year at Christmastime, and Terry had come in for the wedding. Of course. Tris had been her best friend in high school, and there was no way she wasn't going to be there when she finally tied the knot.

"Are you going to decorate for Christmas?" Tris asked cheerfully as they started to put their painting things away.

"It's coming, isn't it? Should we wait until Thanksgiving is here?"

"Goodness, the stores had Christmas displays up in August. We're really behind the times if we're waiting until Thanksgiving." She paused, her hand on a paintbrush. "You heard about Mr. Gregory, didn't you?"

"The township worker?" He'd been the township worker for years. Since she was a little girl. In fact, she couldn't remember anyone else working for the township. He drove around in his truck, waved at them, and gave the leaves he picked up along the road to anyone who wanted them.

"Yeah. He's responsible for putting up the Christmas decorations."

"What happened?"

"He's been such a faithful employee."

"I know. He is one of my good memories of this town. In fact, he almost personifies this town."

"He was diagnosed with cancer this summer, and he's been trying to continue to work, because while the health benefits aren't great, they're still something, but he just hasn't had the energy to get the Christmas decorations out. He can still ride around in his truck and make sure the streets are clear, and the sidewalks are tidy, and the garbage is picked up, and that type of thing, but the Christmas decorations are just beyond him, I think."

"So that's why it hasn't been decorated yet?"

"Yeah. He and his wife are really struggling, and I think the town has been taken by surprise because they haven't had to worry about it for...thirty years? Forty years? Something like that. He's just always been there. And it's hard to realize that he's not. Plus, I think he was hoping he would get better."

"We all do. Anytime that happens to us, we're always hoping that our recovery is faster than expected." She'd definitely seen that in her time in residency. Unfortunately, a lot of times the opposite occurred.

Especially with cancer.

"Am I missing any other things in town?" Terry said, figuring that maybe she ought to get caught up with things. She'd been so concerned about getting a house and getting herself settled that she hadn't really taken the time to catch up on the town gossip.

"I suppose there is a ton, but I don't even know where to start. I hate to do all the gloom and doom stuff."

"That's to be expected. Although, your wedding was a highlight last year."

"It was. The very best. And Fisher is awesome. Being married is better than I expected." She smiled, and there might have been a little blush on her cheeks. "You know Donna Knaus who runs the diner?"

Terry nodded.

"Her niece has been sick. And Jared Smith's cousin's husband left her, and she has four kids to raise by herself."

"That's terrible."

"Yeah. It was a shock to the town, because he always seemed like such a good guy, but I guess he just couldn't take the pressure of being a husband and father,"

"Or he was lured away by something that looked better."

"Yes, exactly."

They were quiet for a moment, realizing that anything could happen to anyone.

"I guess I should warn you that Mrs. Tucker is going to be looking for someone to chronicle the spate of Secret Saint things that have been happening around town. I think pretty much everyone in town has told her no, so you're fresh blood. Just warning you."

"Chronicle the Secret Saint occurrences?"

"Yeah. It's like a Secret Santa, only I think most of the town is tired of the commercialization of Christmas, and they're trying to get back to the whole reason that we celebrate, which is Jesus. So, rather than calling it Secret Santa, they've decided to call it Secret Saint."

"Oh." She had been disillusioned with Christmas lately as well. It seemed so commercialized, with the holiday season being crazy, that she had mostly checked out. It was even better to try to point people back to the reason they celebrated in the first place though, so she could get on board with that.

"The town has its own social media page, and she's looking for someone to do weekly posts, or more often, if she can twist their arm hard enough to get them to post more."

"How do you find out about these things?" She didn't want to do the social media page posts for the town. She figured she'd be busy enough trying to get a practice off the ground and work with the people who would be her patients, her neighbors and friends and fellow townspeople, but she also wanted to be an active part of the community. That was part of what made small towns great, no doubt. People being willing to jump in and help. Picking up where other people wouldn't and taking care of each other. And what a positive message to have every day on social media. Talking about the good things that were happening around town for once, instead of just the bad things that made the news.

"Oh, you'll find out about them. I guess there hasn't been any since you came, but usually there is at least one a week, sometimes two."

"How long has it been happening?"

"Since about the time the stores started putting the Christmas decorations up in their displays. So, the end of August, the beginning of September? I'm not sure exactly, but maybe we missed some. Because a few of them have only been caught just by chance as people started putting two and two together."

"What do you mean?" Terry asked, perplexed.

"Well, there's been money donated to local students to help with their education costs, and our annual mistletoe hop was almost fully funded by an anonymous source. Now, it's a little bit harder to put those two together, but when Mrs. Sobel was in the hospital with her granddaughter, you know her daughter was tragically killed in a car accident, and she's raising her granddaughter on Social Security. Anyway, when she was in the hospital, someone anonymously paid for room and board at the closest hotel. There was just a note at the front desk that said Merry Christmas, Secret Saint. I think that's when we started calling them the Secret Saint episodes."

"Well. Whoever it is must be rich."

"Yeah, I mean there's been little things too, like putting money in parking meters and someone being asked to man a hot chocolate and doughnut stand. The person didn't know who was asking them to do it, but they paid them handsomely, and the whole town got free hot chocolate and doughnuts. It was a really fantastic day back in October."

"And no one knows who does it?"

"Nope. No one's been able to figure it out."

Terry thought for a bit. It had to be one of the people who lived in one of the big mansions down the mountainside. Perhaps someone who had a horse ranch down there. There were several of those, with horses that were worth millions of dollars. Thoroughbreds or other horses. She knew that the horse industry had big money, but usually they didn't make their money with the horses. They brought it into the industry because of what they did.

Regardless, the possibilities were almost endless, and she would have no idea of how to start digging around to figure it out. She'd become a doctor and not an investigator for a reason.

They finished rinsing the brushes out and turned the lights of the small clinic off as they walked out. "I really do appreciate your help," she said, putting her arm around her friend as they walked out.

"My pleasure. You know it's always good to see an old friend, and I'm ecstatic that you're back in town. And to stay. I just couldn't imagine anything better. Except, maybe I wouldn't mind you being as happy as I am. We need to find you someone."

"No way!" Terry said emphatically. She didn't want anyone trying to matchmake for her. "I had a few relationships, nothing that stuck for more than a month or two, and I'm not the slightest bit interested right now. I'm trying to start my business and reestablish connections with my family and friends here. A relationship is not on my list of priorities."

"You know, you're not getting any younger."

"I realize that." And boy, did she ever. It felt like it had taken her forever to get educated enough to actually start practicing medicine.

She felt like half her life was gone. And it very well could be if she died young. Looking back, she wasn't sure it was worth all that time, but at the same time, she loved what she did, and she knew she would love it even more in her small town.

"Do you have plans for Thanksgiving?" Tris asked as they stepped out into the cool November day.

"I'll probably eat at my mom's, although we'll talk about it on Sunday. I'll finally be able to start making her Sunday afternoon dinners again."

"If you want to sit beside us in church, come on up, there's always a spot beside me for you. And if you find out that your family is not doing Thanksgiving, you're welcome to eat with mine. Actually, I'm eating with Fisher."

"All right. I appreciate that. It's always nice to have a backup plan. It's not exactly the kind of day that you want to spend by yourself."

"Agreed. And watch out for Mrs. Tucker," Tris said as she lifted a hand and smiled, waving a bit before she walked jauntily away.

Chapter Nine

For a small town, Mistletoe Meadows sure did have a lot of things going on, and Terry was extremely curious about the whole Secret Saint thing. It almost seemed like it had to be a group of people. Maybe that was why they hadn't figured out who it was, because it was a bunch of people working together.

But it wasn't just about money either, although she figured that whoever was doing it had to be rich. Or maybe it was a rich person teamed up with someone who had time on their hands. Since it had to be someone who was able to take the time to do things like get the doughnuts and hot chocolate and figure out who needed money and how they could best help.

Someone who knew the town well. That almost said it had to be someone who lived in town or possibly someone who was related to someone who lived in town. Which opened up an immense amount of people. She could hardly imagine the time it would take to go through all of them trying to figure out who it was.

It didn't sound like she would be able to catch them in the act, since they seemed to get other people, at least in the case of the hot chocolate and doughnuts, to do things for them, although...who had handed out the hot chocolate and doughnuts? Maybe he just said that an anonymous source had contacted him, when it was actually him.

It wasn't a terrible idea, but again, Terry had other things she needed to do and could hardly spend her time thinking about the Secret Saint.

Her clinic wasn't far from Judd's duplex, and Terry had walked to it that morning. In the winter, or if she wanted to stop and get her groceries or something after work, she'd drive her car, but it was not quite a mile and a good way to get exercise.

She stopped at the local butcher shop and grabbed some vegetables and hamburger for supper.

She was tempted to get enough for two, but not only did she not know Judd that well, but she also didn't know his schedule.

He was such an odd person, but...there was something about him that made her curious, she supposed. Or drew her to him. Maybe it was an attraction, but not one that she was going to act on. After all, they had nothing in common except the shared living space.

He didn't seem like a serial killer, and neither was she, so they had that in common as well, she supposed. But two people who were so opposite could hardly find enough common ground to make any attraction between them worthwhile.

On the way home, she nodded to a few people and waved at more. She had no idea who most of them were, but that's what happened in a small town. You just waved at everyone. Either you already knew them or figured out you knew them from somewhere. And if you didn't, you learned who they were somehow, either at a community event or through a friend or relative. That's just how small towns were.

By the time she'd gotten home, she'd realized how out of shape she was. She had been working so hard the last month, she hadn't taken time for exercise, and the mile, especially carrying groceries for half of it, seemed to drag on forever.

She stepped up on the porch, her stomach growling. She had the clinic all ready and just had a few little odds and ends to straighten up, which she could do tomorrow afternoon after church and the meal with her parents.

She walked in, kicking her shoes off at the door and walking down the hall, noticing when she was halfway down that the light in the kitchen was already on.

It had started to get dark outside, and as often was the case in November, it was cold and overcast.

A cozy kitchen with supper on the stove would be just the thing after a long day of working in her clinic getting it ready.

But if the light was on...either Judd was in the kitchen, or he'd forgotten to turn the light out. For some reason, she was hoping that he'd just forgotten to turn it off, not because she didn't want to talk to him, but because...he made her a little nervous with his long silences and odd sense of humor.

Not uncomfortable; she felt totally comfortable around him, which didn't seem to jive with the fact that he made her nervous.

But as she stepped into the kitchen, it was obvious that she was either going to be sharing the space, or she would have to wait to cook her own meal until he was done.

"Good evening," she said, putting a smile on her face and admitting to herself that there was a sort of thrill that went through her to see that he was here. Maybe she just didn't want to be alone. She'd spent plenty of time by herself in various apartments and housing situations over the course of her education, and she had good roommates and bad, but she never lived with a man.

She hadn't thought she was "living" with a man when she asked to rent the other side of his duplex.

This house was not the kind of duplex she was used to.

"Hey. I made some extra if you want some." Judd had turned and looked over his shoulder, and then he nodded to the stove where he had cooked chicken and roasted vegetables.

It smelled divine.

"I can't eat your food. And I bought some of my own, it's just going to take me a little bit to cook it. Is it going to bother you if I'm in here while you are?"

"It doesn't bother me at all, but if that'll wait until tomorrow night, you can cook it then. It's up to you. I'll eat my leftovers tomorrow, but I didn't want to cook without including you."

She nodded her head, her lips working up just a bit. She'd never shared a place with a roommate who had ever said that they hated to cook for just themselves. Sometimes they would cook for others if they had to, and sometimes they traded back and forth, with one person cooking on one day and one person cooking on another day, although the problem with that was sometimes people didn't keep their days or cooked something that was inedible. But it was almost like he made it knowing she would be busy, and he wanted to lighten her load.

"I'm not going to be offended if you say no," he said as he walked over to the cupboard. He paused, then looked back over his shoulder. "Should I get one plate out or two?"

It should be one. She should say one. She didn't want to get into a situation where she ended up doing all the work, because that's what ultimately happened. She was the one who kept her word. She was the one who did what she said she was going to do, and she was the one who ended up cooking and then getting burned by people who dropped their end of the bargain.

But he wasn't offering a bargain. He wasn't telling her that she had to do anything in return.

"I don't think we have to eat together every night."

"I'm not always home this time of night, especially in the summer, but if I'm here, I don't mind cooking, and I don't mind sharing. No reciprocation necessary. It's just an offer."

"All right. No reciprocation necessary, but I'll do it if I happen to be around."

"Sounds good. Although, I figure you'll be working nine to five and not be around much."

"Actually, I can't do it right now, but I'd like to change the clinic hours to Monday through Thursday ten to seven. I feel like those would be better hours for people, and then I would have the morning hours if I needed to add anything, and Fridays if necessary."

"That actually sounds good. I don't know why more doctors don't do that—have hours that are outside the norm."

"Probably because they want to spend the evenings at home with their families. But I don't have that right now, so I can offer it. Eventually I might not be able to, but who knows what the future holds." She didn't want to get into whether or not she would ever get married and have a family. They didn't know each other well enough for that, although if they were going to eat together tonight, she would hopefully know him better than she had.

He pulled two plates out while she put her groceries in the refrigerator and went to the sink to wash her hands.

There was silence between them, but it didn't feel awkward, and she didn't feel the need to fill it. Rather, she looked at him covertly, thinking about what she had thought earlier about the pull that seemed to be between them. At least for her. He wasn't unattractive, but she wouldn't consider him classically handsome. He had deep blue eyes, almost black, which is probably how she got the impression that he was dark. That along with the dark hair and the dark brows that rose over those deep-set eyes.

He wasn't skinny, but she wouldn't label him fat either. His BMI was most definitely under obese, but if he were her patient and she had to give him a recommendation, she would probably tell him that it wouldn't hurt for him to lose a little weight. The same could be said for her. Maybe walking to and from work would help her with that.

Regardless, she didn't find him unattractive and wondered again if renting from him was the best idea.

"I just wanted you to know that I'm still looking for a place, and I won't be here bothering you for long, if I can help it."

Those words just tumbled out of her mouth, without her planning on saying them. But she knew that was for the best. She didn't want to stay here any longer than she had to. He was intriguing and attractive to her, and that was probably dangerous.

Especially since he didn't seem to notice her looking at him and didn't seem the slightest bit interested in looking at her.

He lifted his shoulder, as though it didn't matter to him whether she stayed or left, and went back to the drawer to grab silverware.

She opened a couple of cupboards until she found glasses and walked to the sink. "Is the tap water okay to drink?"

He lifted a big shoulder. "It hasn't killed me yet."

She laughed. Although, the doctor in her wanted to cringe. Lots of people thought that, but sometimes death didn't happen right away. But the changes that led to death, or more likely cancer or some other disease, weren't such that a person could see when they drank water that shouldn't have been drunk or ate something that shouldn't have been eaten. Such as hot chocolate and doughnuts.

She thought again of the Secret Saint. If Judd were more personable, she might think that he might be a good person to keep an eye out for her. If she was actually trying to figure out who it was, but she wasn't. Since Judd did odd jobs all around town and probably ran into a lot of different people in his line of work.

"Excuse me," he said as he set the small casserole dish with chicken in it on the table.

She walked over and grabbed the roasted vegetables. It looked like he might have put olive oil or something on them, and some salt, and they looked perfectly done. Carrots, onions, peppers, and mushrooms.

"These look really good. Did you season them?"

"A little bit of garlic, nothing else. But if you want something, there are a lot of spices in the cupboard, pick your poison."

She laughed, wanting to argue, since spices were often very good for a person. There were very few spices that a person had to eat in moderation and that didn't have some kind of health benefit. In fact, she wasn't sure if there were any.

"Garlic sounds just perfect," she said. She liked simple, and it looked like Judd did too.

The kitchen seemed well lit, but with the darkness outside the windows, it also seemed cozy, not too bright, just perfect for a fall evening together around the table.

"I always pray over my food. I can do it aloud if you want me to, or you can. Or, if that's not you—"

"If you want to, I would appreciate it."

Sometimes she already had food in her mouth by the time she remembered she was supposed to pray. Mostly that happened in residency and med school, where she was eating between studying and taking care of patients and trying to figure out difficult cases and navigate her way through all of that with very little sleep.

She sat down, and he bowed his head. She waited for a beat, looking at him with his head bowed and feeling that stirring in her heart that had happened several times already when she was around Judd.

"Lord God, thank you for the beautiful fall day You gave us and the way You provided for us. Thank you for a warm home and good company. Please bless the food and help us to use it to bring honor and glory to You. Amen."

His prayer was sincere, and it felt like it was coming from his heart, while not corny or sentimental.

Okay, so he'd impressed her. Silly that a prayer should do that, but it did.

"You must be used to cooking for yourself," she began as he grabbed one piece of chicken and she took some vegetables.

"Yeah," he said and then lapsed into silence again.

Did he know that it was his turn to make a comment or ask a question to keep the conversation flowing?

Maybe he just needed to get warmed up.

She waited until he picked the vegetables up before she grabbed a piece of chicken.

"This looks a little crusted, did you put some kind of seed things on it?" she asked, not really because she cared, although she was curious. It smelled so good.

"Just something I've made up myself. Some breadcrumbs and I dipped it in egg. And a few other seasonings. It works for me."

"It smells delicious to me," she said, feeling awkward. The conversation just felt stilted, like he didn't want to talk, and she couldn't pull words out of him. Her voice sounded too bright and cheerful for the winter evening.

"You don't need to feel like you have to talk, if you don't want to. Although you can." He paused and then said, "How did things go at the clinic?"

He had given her permission not to answer before he even asked the question. And she appreciated that, but she appreciated even more that he didn't sound like he was asking the question because he was trying to make conversation. It sounded like he was asking the question because he was truly interested in what she might say.

She wasn't sure how she could put her finger on the difference, but it was there. Again, she knew from her work, not necessarily her studies, that sometimes the brain-heart combination was more powerful than the intellect.

Hmm. Somehow Judd had a way of touching her that made her want to draw closer to him.

"We got all the walls painted in the waiting room, and I have things organized in my office. I took some of my medical books and put them on shelves, although so much stuff is online that it was more for decoration than for any actual necessity."

"Doctors, too, huh?"

She laughed a little. "We're not immune."

He didn't say anything more, and after she chewed a bite of chicken, she said, "I went through the exam rooms, there's three of them, and familiarized myself with where everything is. I just feel a little restless, you know? Like, maybe I should be doing something more."

"I think that's normal. You're settling in."

"Yeah. It was very nice not to have to cook this evening. I don't really enjoy it."

"I find it soothing. Just something to do after a long day of work. I think about what will nourish my body, and it's just mindless work that you can sit and think about whatever you want to."

"I get the feeling that you do a lot of thinking."

"I think your feeling is correct," he said with a little smile that maybe was slightly self-effacing.

"There's nothing wrong with that."

"Well, thanks," he said, and this time, there was irony in his voice.

"Sorry. Maybe I have a tendency to talk too much. I do like to talk things out to work them through, to figure out what I want to do, especially issues or problems where the answer isn't obvious to me."

"I guess I like to figure things out in my head before I open my mouth. So often what comes out of my mouth isn't ready."

"I guess that's where we differ, because the stuff that comes out of my mouth isn't ready either," she said with a laugh. "But that's why I say it. I guess maybe so I can hear it and think about it."

"I see," he said, nodding his head thoughtfully. Like he really was paying attention to what she said and was chewing on her words.

She thought about the Secret Saint and about asking him to help her, but something held her back. She hadn't been asked to do the social media posts and maybe she wouldn't be, and when she started on her clinic, she probably wouldn't have time to give any thought to that anyway.

"It seems odd, you going to school for years and studying to become a doctor, and then you end up coming back here. I would have thought you would want to go do something big somewhere. Is there something else that drew you back?"

It was an intelligent question, and thankfully, one that was fairly easy for her to answer.

"The whole reason I became a doctor is because I wanted to have a clinic here in my own hometown. That was my dream. Not really becoming a doctor. I know that's strange and almost opposite from what normal people do. But that was my goal. That was the whole thought behind everything I've done."

"You don't really care to be a doctor?" he asked, sounding mildly surprised.

"I do! I found that I love it! Although, I think you can love whatever you do, you know? You just decide that you're going to enjoy your life. You're going to make the most of what you have and have fun doing it. And it's a mindset thing."

"Yeah. I can agree with that. Think positive."

"Yeah. It goes beyond thinking positive, because you can think pretty preposterous positive things, like we're going to have Florida summer weather all winter long. You know?"

"Wow. The climate alarmists would be here with bells on if that were to happen. I definitely don't want that."

"It would kind of ruin the small-town vibe, wouldn't it?"

"It would make Christmas not as fun either," he said, and again his tone was mild, although it was laced with a note of humor.

"Anyway, coming back here is almost like a dream come true."

"But you weren't planning on living in a duplex," he said, lifting a brow at her as though daring her to contradict that.

"I don't know. I guess I never really thought about where I would live. I suppose my plan was to move back in with my parents and help them while doing my clinic."

"Didn't you want to buy your own home?"

"I'm single, by myself. What's the point of buying a big old house? Especially when my parents live in a big old house and have plenty of room."

"Why didn't you do that then?"

"Maybe you haven't heard, but my brother Gilbert and his wife have moved back in with their three kids because Sally had cancer, and it's returned. It's in her bones, she's...taking treatments, but it doesn't look good."

"I see." He nodded, looking sad but not surprised. She got the feeling that he already knew that, and that's what made her add, "I could have moved in there anyway, but it just felt like it would be crowded, you know? It also felt like I would be taking attention away from my brother, who needs it. He needs Mom right now, his kids do, too, and Mom has a tendency to want to nurture everyone around her. I'm just one less person she needs to nurture and worry about."

"Oh, I'm sure she still probably worries about you whether you're in her house or not."

"I imagine you're probably right," she said. "Mom always said that I would understand better when I had children. Although I don't know if that's going to happen."

"Why wouldn't it?" he asked easily, and she realized again that it was so easy to talk to him.

"Well, I'm single. And I don't sleep around, so it's not going to happen unless I get married, and since there are no prospects, at all." She shrugged her shoulders, tilting her head. "I just don't see it."

"You're coming back to your hometown. Surely there's a whole new dating pool."

"Do you realize how small our town is? And most people our age are married." As she said that, she realized she was staring at someone who wasn't.

That was awkward. She looked quickly back down at her plate, but not before she thought that he probably had been thinking about the same thing.

He didn't say anything, so as she industriously cut her vegetables into extremely tiny pieces, she said, "Why haven't you married?" She felt pleased with the way her voice didn't sound as flustered as she felt.

"I guess I just haven't met the right one yet," he said.

Chapter Ten

Judd wanted to put his head in his hand. What a cliché. Everyone said that. Yet there he was, spouting off nonsense. He wanted to sound more intelligent. After all, she was a doctor.

But he couldn't change what he was. Just a man, with little education, who did his best to try to be a blessing wherever God put him.

He had never felt the need to move, but he had always felt the need to do more. And along with that, his desire to not put himself out front, or show people what he was doing, or brag about it.

He hated that, and it made him feel as terrible as helping people made him feel good.

Regardless, he had the most interesting woman sitting at his supper table that he'd ever spoken with in his entire life.

He admired her in school, obviously knew who she was, but hadn't really considered that they ever might talk. Even though they spent six years in the same homeroom.

But now, now he not only cooked for her, she was sitting at his table eating, and yet...he couldn't think of anything intelligent to say.

And he definitely didn't want to talk about his nonexistent love life. She would probably think he was some kind of loser who couldn't keep a girl, because he didn't have the excuse of spending his entire adult life in school, being trained to be a doctor. As she did. It made sense that someone as interesting as she was wasn't married.

With her golden-brown hair, and her brilliant blue eyes, the color of the September sky, and her wide mouth that broke into a grin easily, he thought she was beautiful.

But she was already looking for another place to live and obviously didn't want to spend any more time with him than she had to. He didn't want to make a fool out of himself.

Also, having the doctor in on his scheme might be beneficial, but he wasn't sure he could trust her even though Wilson said she was good. Or maybe it was himself he couldn't trust.

"You were just telling me about all the eligible people in town," she said, and then, to his everlasting gratitude, she changed the subject. "You did an excellent job on this meal."

"It's very simple, easy to make, but so, so good."

"You'll have to let me know what your spice blends are. I could eat this every day."

"I could make it every day and often do. I cooked a little more chicken than I normally do, but sometimes I'll buy a family pack and just eat it that week."

"Wow. I don't know if I could eat it that often." She sighed. "Why do we care about what we eat? Why is it such a struggle?"

"Just one of those things that help shape our character. At least that's how I look at it. Because you're right, God could have just made us eat grass or whatever. Think about cows, their diet hardly ever changes. Fresh grass in the spring and summer and maybe fall, and dry grass in the winter. Hope you like grass."

"You're right. And they never get tired of it."

"Although, I can say that in the spring when you first let them out on grass, they can't wait to get in there and belly up, and stuff themselves. You can see that they enjoy it. But after they've been on grass for a month or so, if you stick a hay bale in there, they'll eat that. It's interesting, like they like the new thing. Now, once they've eaten a little bit and had the novelty, they go back to the fresh grass, if they get a choice."

"You know a lot about cows. Wow. Did you live on a farm?"

"I grew up on one."

"Oh, you did?" she asked, and he felt like she was getting a little too close for comfort to things he didn't want to talk about. At least not yet.

"We went to school all of our lives, and you never even knew where I lived. I suppose I should be offended over that."

"A lot of people would," she said easily. She'd been done for a while but had set her fork down beside her plate and just sat there, like some dinner table conversation was welcome.

"I guess if you want dessert, you'll have to make it."

"If you're cooking the main course, I'll be responsible for dessert, but... I usually don't eat it at every meal."

"Same. In fact, I never do. Unless I buy it somewhere, since I'm just not cooking something sweet for myself."

"So you're not a baker?"

"You read between the lines and understood that I would if I could, but I can't." He wasn't sure what it was, but talking to her just made him feel humorous. And he liked that he didn't have to spell everything out for her, but that she could figure things out. Although, that wasn't good for him keeping his secret identity from her.

"I was getting that impression. My mom is a baker, and I cooked a lot when I was growing up, but as I started to get into high school and of course college and med school and then residency... I stopped, first of all because of time constraints, but nothing that you make in the dessert category is good for you."

"But you want to be able to live a little. You don't want to spend your entire life in austerity and deprive yourself of everything good."

"I agree that there should be moderation. The Bible says so."

"Let everything be done in moderation."

"Isn't eating part of everything?"

"Good point. I guess sometimes people try to take the Bible and apply it to things it doesn't apply to, but you're right, it says everything, and we can assume that God actually means everything."

"I think that's a good assumption, but regardless, we all know that excessive amounts of sugar are bad for you, and moderate amounts of sugar are not good for you, and no amounts of sugar are the best, so you can take that and do with it what you will."

"Most people take that and ignore it," he said, taking a sip of his water and feeling full and satisfied and happy like he hadn't in a long time. Doing kind things for people did satisfy his soul in a deep and meaningful way, but this was more...maybe man's need for companionship. Someone who understood him. Not that Terry fit that bill. They barely knew each other, but she seemed to get what he said and not be intimidated by his need to warm up to people before he started chatting.

At least, if she was intimidated, she did a good job of hiding it.

"It sounds like this is going to become a regular thing?" he started. "But I don't want you to feel pressure. I understand that with your job, you might have to work late some days, and the idea that you might feel like you're dropping the ball and didn't provide a meal when you were supposed to—"

"I can't believe I'm saying this, but I wouldn't mind splitting the cooking duties, and we negate the issue you just brought up if you cook Monday through Thursday and I do Friday Saturday and Sunday when my workload is lighter. I can't say that I would never open up the clinic for someone who needed me, but I should at least be able to get a couple meals on the table."

"All right. I don't want you to do it if you don't really want to." He had gotten the idea that she was reluctant.

"I've done this with people who didn't pull their fair share. You know? You have someone who's assigned to take out the trash and someone who is assigned to do dishes or whatever, and it seems like I'm the only one who ever cleans up or does anything, and it gets annoying."

"I see. Well, maybe that's just because you were young and the people you were with were the same age. I've been cleaning up after myself for a while now, and cooking as well. I think I can probably be responsible for meals."

She looked a little abashed and apologized immediately. "I'm sorry. I didn't mean to imply that you weren't responsible."

"No. I didn't take it that you did. I got the idea that you've been burned."

"That's exactly right."

He pushed back away from the table, loathe to end their conversation but knowing that he had some things that he needed to do that evening.

"We might have to revisit this in the summer, when I'm busy with mowing grass. But for now, I usually quit by dark, and if you're going to change your hours and close your clinic at six, it'll be seven until you're ready to eat."

"Especially if I walk home. Which I want to try to do. If I were my patient, I would tell myself to lose a little weight."

"If I were your patient, you'd tell me to lose weight too."

She grinned and didn't bother to deny it. He wouldn't want her to lie to him. And he was glad that she hadn't felt the need to deny his words somehow, when they both knew that they were true.

"That dessert I don't cook sometimes happens to jump into my freezer as ice cream."

He took both of their plates and walked them to the sink. Doing the dishes wasn't hard, and while two was twice as many as one, the conversation and company at the table made up for it. He hadn't realized how nice it could be.

"I think I'm down for ice cream as well. Although more in the summer."

"Yeah, it's holiday baking that gets me now."

"The hot chocolate and doughnuts," she said, and he was glad he had his back to her, facing the sink.

Had she heard about that? Did she mention it because she suspected him? Surely not. He had gotten completely away with it, even people who lived in town didn't have any idea. She couldn't have come into town and figured everything out in just a couple days. There was just no way.

But she was a smart woman. He had to give her that.

"Hot doughnuts, fresh out of the grease, are the best," he said. Completely ignoring the idea that she might have known and perhaps was looking to get a reaction out of him. But if she was, why had she waited until he turned around not looking at her so she couldn't watch his face?

He didn't like hiding things from people. That wasn't his goal, and this wasn't anything bad. He just didn't like to be out in front of people, grabbing a lot of spotlight and attention for the good things he wanted to do. He had considered that perhaps it was good to be an example to people, but more of him wanted to just keep a low profile and not put himself out there.

But he wasn't going to worry about it. If she knew, she knew and he would deal with it. Otherwise, he would enjoy his time with her until she found a new place.

It was funny though, that most of him did not want her to go. He hadn't been sure when Amy suggested that she stay with him that he wanted a housemate or that he wanted to go along with their matchmaking efforts, but... He found Terry was even better than Amy had said.

"It's chilly this evening, and I thought I might spend an hour in my living room with the fire. You're welcome to join me if you'd like."

He hadn't been planning on building a fire at all; he'd been planning on going out and getting started on the job he knew had needed to be done for a while. He just hadn't had a chance. It was a kind of job that was going to take more than one night. Thankfully, Wilson was willing to help him, and they had a plan. Wilson wasn't going to be in town until after midnight. Typically from twelve to four were the best times when everything was shut down. They could get started a little earlier if they weren't going to be working right on the main street of town.

"That sounds really nice. Do you do that often?" she asked as she finished wiping the table and stood beside him, wringing the rag out.

"I do it a good bit in December. It's like Christmas to me. Sometimes in January, just to take the chill off the house, but by February, I'm ready for spring and I'm not really interested in fires at that point."

"That sounds perfect," she said. "I have some work I need to do tonight, but I'll definitely take a rain check on that if you don't mind."

Tempted to tell her that she could bring her work over—he wasn't inviting her because he needed someone to talk to—he didn't. Instead, he just nodded. "Any time I'm over there with the fire, you're welcome to come over."

"Might you have a date at some point? I'm sure you don't want to be interrupted."

"That hasn't happened yet," he said, wondering how they got back to that subject. He thought he'd dodged it nicely the first time. He didn't expect her to circle around, although she did not seem like the kind of woman who'd give up easily.

But that was okay, because he wasn't that kind of man.

Chapter Eleven

"Did you see what happened?" Tris asked Terry as soon as they saw each other at church. Which was when Terry pulled into the parking lot. Tris had been waiting to pounce on her.

"No? What happened?" Terry asked, looking around, wondering what she missed. It had to be something huge.

"Someone put the Christmas decorations up last night on Main Street!" she said, her voice a whisper, although Terry didn't know why.

"Is this a secret?"

"No?" Tris said, looking at her strangely.

"I just wondered why you are shouting in a whisper."

"Oh. I guess it's just so...crazy, exciting."

"Secret Saint," Dolly said as she stepped up to them.

"Yeah. It has to be him. Her. I think it's a girl," Tris said, looking smug.

"Well, if it's a girl, she is strong. Especially if she was working alone."

"You think the decorations are heavy?" Tris asked.

"I know they are. I helped put them away last year. They're definitely heavy."

"Noted. Although, I don't know why I need to know that."

"That wouldn't be something that you would need to know, unless you're going to work on putting them up all night, and then you might want to spend a few weeks at the gym building up to it," Terry said as she grabbed her Bible and notebook and got out of the car.

She was so happy to be back at her hometown church, even though the pastor was different than the one she grew up with. She heard he was really good. Her entire family had said that, and she had looked forward to the day she got to hear him, going to church, chatting with her family, and then looking forward to opening her clinic the next day.

Maybe she'd walk through it one last time, just make sure everything was in order.

"Terry McBride!" Mrs. Tucker said as she hurried up to the three friends.

Tris gave her a scared look, and Dolly said, "I just realized that I need to go back and make sure my husband's okay. I'll talk to you later." She started to step away, waving. "Hi, Mrs. Tucker!" she said as she hurried in the opposite direction.

"I'd love to stay and chat too, but I'm teaching Sunday school, and I better go get my lesson ready," Tris said as she also hurried off in a different direction. But not in the direction of Mrs. Tucker.

"Hi, Mrs. Tucker," Terry said, making a mental note to thank her sister and her friend for standing with her through thick and thin, even if that involved Mrs. Tucker.

"Terry McBride. You are back among us," Mrs. Tucker said, tapping her arm with the clipboard that she carried. She was obviously old-school, since it was not an iPad. "Or so your family tells me. They do know, right?"

"They do." Her words were easy, although she couldn't help the note of suspicion in her voice. And maybe a little bit of distance. But after the reaction that Dolly and Tris had had, she felt like maybe she should have run too.

"Well, sometimes people come back, just because they got fired or had some kind of scandal, and their small town welcomes them with open arms, loves them and cares for them and exclaims how happy they are to have them back, then when things die down, they leave us again. Is that going to be you?" she asked, looking at Terry over the rim of her glasses which were perched on the edge of her nose.

"I have every intention of staying here until I die, and even then I'm not planning on leaving if there's room in the graveyard for me."

"We'll just cremate you and spread your ashes somewhere close," Mrs. Tucker said breezily.

"I don't want to be cremated," she said. There was just something about cremation that didn't seem to be biblical. She didn't have a verse to quote, but the principle of respecting the body because it was made in the image of God just seemed too much to ignore.

She wasn't quite sure how she got on the subject of cremation with Mrs. Tucker.

"Well, regardless, you're alive and kicking, and that means you are prime game for me. I have a job I wanted to ask if you are interested in doing."

"I'd love to serve in the church, if you want," Terry said easily. Knowing that was true. She couldn't do some things, like if Mrs. Tucker wanted her to lead the trumpet section or replace the roof.

"Well, this doesn't exactly have to do with church. I just haven't been able to catch up with you since you got here."

"It's only been three days," Terry said.

"I know, but usually I work faster than this. It's just the season, you know. I have family coming in, and I was trying to get everything arranged in town to make sure I don't miss anything, and I have something that's been going on, and I need you to help me with it."

"Well, tell me what it is," Terry said, remembering that she'd been warned and realizing that she never decided whether she was going to accept the position or not. Did she want to do it?

"We have a position open for social media poster. Now, you're freshly back, so you might not know that someone has been doing anonymous good works around town, and they've signed several notes calling themselves the Secret Saint. I want you to get on the town's social media page and post details. You can even speculate on who you think it might be and why."

"All right, is that it?"

"I think that's more than enough. We just had another hit yesterday last night sometime. When I left Main Street last night, there were no Christmas decorations up on the telephone poles, but this morning, both sides of Main Street are completely decorated, and I know it wasn't Mr. Gregory, he's had cancer and can barely get out of bed, although the township is too kind to fire him."

"Maybe that's because his health insurance wasn't very good and they feel bad about it," Terry surmised but was totally guessing, since she didn't know.

"That could be. Good point." Mrs. Tucker looked up then made a mark on her notebook. "Regardless, I'm here to try to fill the position of social media poster. I'd like to have a picture with every post if I can, and while I know you're busy with your new practice, I know that you want to give back to the community, and this would be a great way to do that."

"I see. All right, the pictures might be kind of hard since I'm planning on being in my clinic all day long. I can't get pictures and stuff."

"You can put your contact info in, and I would suggest making up an entirely new email account just for this, so people don't get your actual email account and spam it or try to hack it. Regardless, they can send you pictures. You can ask for them, and you will find that our small town hasn't changed at all. People are still eager to help."

"All right. That's good to know. I guess."

"All right, it's settled. Give me your phone number, and I will text you all the information you need in order to get into our account and get set up as an administrator."

"All right," Terry said, thinking that she had meant to say that she was going to think about it and get back to her, but somehow that didn't happen. Had she not been clear or maybe not fast enough?

Before she knew it, Terry had given Mrs. Tucker her information, and Mrs. Tucker, true to type, had texted her the information to get on the social media page within five minutes.

Terry walked slowly toward the church, thinking that if she was going to survive in the small town, she needed to remember where her backbone was. Although, Mrs. Tucker could have asked her to do anything, and she probably would have agreed. Just because she liked helping out and she knew that it was essential to a small town's viability.

She was still thinking as the sound of...bells caught her ear. Bells?

She turned her head around first to the right and then to the left, trying to pick up where the noise was coming from.

There were kids on the back of the wagon, and suddenly she realized Amy was standing with them, leading them in song. It was a fun hymn, and Terry felt her toe tapping as she listened, even as her eyes took in the scene. There were two horses pulling the wagon, two black horses like the ones that Terry had seen at Amy's sanctuary that she had said belonged to someone who was renting space.

And then, she did a double take, because it sure looked like Judd in the wagon seat, driving the horses.

She blinked, trying to process that information.

Judd had left the duplex that morning before she had gotten out of bed. She heard the front door close and his steps on the front porch since her bed was right next to the window.

She figured he was going to work or something and felt a pang of disappointment. His prayer had been so good and inspiring yesterday, but...apparently he wasn't going to church.

It was okay, a lot of people didn't, but in order for her to continue to be a good Christian, she needed a weekly, or sometimes multiple times a week, reminder of what she was supposed to be working on and doing in her life. If she didn't deliberately try to stay close to the Lord, she would fall away. It was just Murphy's Law. Which applied to Christians as well as to non-Christians.

But not only was he intending to go to church, he got up early so that he could apparently go get the horses that were owned by someone, Amy hadn't said who, and bring them down to town, and then pick kids up with them.

What a clever way to get children to go to church, first of all, and secondly, what a fun sight. It was true, there was no snow, so he wasn't driving a sleigh, but...he had said he had grown up on a farm. She remembered that from last night, and she wanted to ask where it was, but she got sidetracked, because she'd been embarrassed that she'd gone to school with him for thirteen years and didn't even know where he lived. It was a small town. She definitely should have known.

But whatever farm he had lived on, they must have had horses. He seemed to handle them well, or maybe it was just because they were so old.

Regardless, the sight made her smile, as the wagon, decorated with greenery and red ribbons that flowed in the breeze, shook a bit as the kids tumbled off, smiling and laughing and still singing.

Her sister Amy jumped off behind them, and then she threw a hand up to Judd, who nodded at her before clucking to his horses and they started off, their bells jingling.

Terry had not been expecting to see anything like that, and she couldn't believe how it made her feel. Surprised, sure, but warm and happy, that there were people who would donate their time and abilities and even a team of horses to get kids to church.

If there was any hope for their country, they really needed to be teaching children a biblical foundation. After all, they weren't getting it anywhere else.

It was a great need, but Judd had not struck her as the kind of person who worked with kids.

Although Amy was perfect for it. Bubbly and happy, with boundless energy. Although, she did seem to be more worried than she used to. Of course. Adulthood had a tendency to do that to people. And Terry was sure being responsible for all of those animals had to have a stress all of its own.

As she slowly walked into the sanctuary, nodding at the people she knew, she thought about the man that she'd been talking to the night before at supper. He shared supper with her, cooked enough for two, not even knowing that she would be home, just knowing it was a good thing to do.

And then, getting up early this morning and taking the kids to church in a horse-drawn wagon. It was something that he would have had to spend a good bit of time and effort preparing.

"Aunt Terry! You're here!" Lucas, Gilbert's oldest son, came running to her and wrapped his arms around her followed closely by his younger brother and sister.

"Did you guys ride to church on the wagon?" she asked, not having seen them.

"No. But Mr. Judd will give rides after church before he takes everyone else home for those of us who come with our parents."

So it was like a bus ministry. He wasn't picking up regular churchgoing kids, he was actually picking up kids whose parents weren't here.

Wow. It was even more than what she thought.

"All right then. That sounds like fun!"

"He'll take big people too," little Robert volunteered, and Terry had to smile at his word for adults—big people.

"You should go, Aunt Terry!" Marissa said, standing with her arms around her waist and her head buried in her stomach. "And I'm glad you're back."

"I'm glad too. I should get to see you guys a lot more."

Typically she would come in on her day off, which was often a day during the week, and sometimes the kids were at school. But she had tried to make a point of knowing them and having a relationship with them as much as she could, especially since she'd started working at the practice in Richmond. Being a resident and going through med school didn't give her a whole lot of time.

"All right, guys," Gilbert said, appearing at her side, smiling but looking tired and haggard. "Let's get ourselves inside. It's almost time to start."

The kids gave Terry one last hug and tore off into the church.

"Mom said you were thinking about moving in with her. I hope I didn't scare you off," he said, falling into step beside her and walking at a much more sedate pace than his children had.

"You didn't scare me, but right now, you need Mom. Your kids need her, and you guys need that space. I know I wouldn't have been a problem. I'm not trying to say that I was or that you would have thought of me that way, I just wanted to make sure that you guys remain center stage. Does that make sense?"

"It does. But I feel bad. I didn't intend to...move in with my mom at thirty..." His voice trailed off, and she could see the grief and tiredness on his very person almost pouring off him, and she didn't have to ask how Sally was doing, although she was going to anyway because it was just good to ask about her. That way, Gilbert could go home today and tell her, in case she didn't make it to the Sunday meal.

Chapter Twelve

"How's she doing?" Terry asked, taking a breath and bracing herself.

"She's actually still in Richmond. They admitted her to the hospital last night. Just... Low numbers and not what they want to see. She insisted I come home and go to church with the kids and try to keep things as normal as possible, but someone's going to need to tell them."

"Or prepare them." She did know that they didn't necessarily need to know that Sally was dying, although, maybe. Did a person ever really get prepared for that kind of thing?

"Do you think it would be better to just spring it on them?"

"I think they probably know it's serious. But I don't know. That's not really something I'm trained for as a doctor, but I guess I would say, lots of times you get things sprung on you, car accidents, and those types of things, where you just have to deal. And there's a possibility that she could pull through. I guess I wouldn't be all gloom and doom."

"I try not to be, but it's been discouraging, because we've had nothing but bad news."

"I'm sorry," she said, linking her arm through his as they walked through the vestibule and into the sanctuary.

"Don't be sorry. I know God has this for a reason. He has us walking through these hard things and gives them to us because He thinks we can handle them and that they will make us better and that will bring glory to Him, but that doesn't mean they're not hard."

It sounded like her brother had all the right ideas. And she didn't have any better ideas than what he had, and she didn't know what to do to help him.

"Just because I'm not living with you doesn't mean I won't drop everything I have and come help you if I need to. You just say the word, okay?"

"Yeah. I know I can count on you. And it is kind of reassuring to have a doctor in the family."

"Not that I have any experience with oncology." Other than a little stint in residency, which was more depressing than she wanted to admit.

There was some interesting research coming out, but they were years away from anything resembling a one-hundred-percent cure or even something that would help most of the time. Chemo was so terrible.

Speaking of chemo, she saw Dr. Vivik and his wife off to the side, moving slowly to their seats. She hadn't spoken to him since she'd come back, and after saying a few more words to Gilbert, she hurried to greet the doctor.

He had built a practice over thirty years in her hometown. He had been her doctor when she had been little. And she had great admiration and respect for him. He'd known how to handle the small-town people because he was one himself. He'd known what they liked and didn't like, and he did his best to try to keep them as healthy as he could.

He'd shared with her that he had ups and downs, but that it had been more than worth it.

However, with the physical issues of his wife, he looked older and tired and so different from the last time she'd seen him, which had been less than a month ago.

"Dr. Vivik, Mrs. Vivik," she said as she stepped out of the aisle, slightly in front of their pew so they could see her.

"Terry! I've been thinking about you," Doc said, glancing at his wife, who was smiling up at her. She had been active in the community, especially with children. She'd been the librarian for a while and a nurse in his practice as well.

Terry remembered her from both roles.

"I meant to tell you that there are decorations in the closet, and you can help yourself. My wife and I discussed it, and we took everything that we wanted, just a few personal pictures and my books from the office. Although, I suppose I could have left them there for you. It's not that I'm going to need them in retirement."

"If you want to bring them back, that's fine, or keep them. I'm fine with either one." Most of the information in his books would have been obsolete, but they might have been interesting to look at now or in the future. Just to see how things had changed. Doctors were constantly finding new things out, new research was being uncovered, and best practices today would be worse practices ten years from now.

"I'll think about it. Maybe if I get around to it. We've been pretty busy with treatments and stuff, but Peggy is doing well," he said, looking lovingly at his wife, but there was no hiding the worry in his eyes. "I definitely prefer to be on your side of the lab coat. Being the patient stinks."

"Having a doctor for a husband is not exactly a walk in the park either, especially when you're going through something like this. He is constantly telling me what I should or shouldn't be doing."

"It might be the husband in him more than the doctor," Terry said fondly.

"You could be right," Mrs. Vivik said, giving her husband an affectionate glance.

She was obviously wearing a wig, but her brown eyes still twinkled, and while the red on her cheeks and lips were because of the makeup she applied, and her cheekbones stood out starkly where they never used to, there was an indomitable spirit about her that made Terry think that if someone could beat this, she could.

"Cancer is such an epidemic in our country. If I had to go back and do things again, I almost wish I could have studied it, to try to come up with some kind of cure."

"Seems like prevention is the best cure," Terry said, even though she knew that that was not true one hundred percent of the time. There were people who did everything right and still got cancer. Children who ended up with a dread disease. How did one prevent that type of cancer? "I have to admit that the research part interests me as well, but I love working with people, and I don't think I would have been happy in a lab."

"No, unless I felt like I was doing good for the world," Doc said, and she supposed she could agree with that. Even though she loved seeing people all day long, if she had to choose between that and being able to figure out a cure for cancer, she'd choose the cure. And give up what she felt like she needed in order to survive—contact with everyone.

"We have a week off from treatments, so if you want to give me a call, you can."

"Unless we need to make an emergency trip to Richmond, which we needed to do a couple of weeks ago," Mrs. Vivik said.

The pianist started to play a Christmas carol, and Terry looked around at the church which was almost full.

"I better go find a seat," she said as she saw her sister waving at her before the pew filled up with her other sister and brother, and there was not any room left for her.

"Looks like we're full, or I'd invite you to sit with us," Doc said.

"You've already been so good to me," she said, meaning it from the bottom of her heart. Doc was a good man. Unselfish, and not after money, but truly interested in how he could help people. It was the kind of person she wanted to be, and she hoped it was the kind of person she was.

"My patients couldn't have a more deserving person take over. I wouldn't have guessed when you were a little kid in pigtails that you'd grow up to take the practice over from me, but I'm proud of you," he said, and that warmed her heart, to know that what she had done had pleased him.

She gave a wave and looked around the church, trying to figure out where she could sit. She didn't have to sit with someone she knew, but she'd been going to church by herself and sitting alone for so long that she kind of wanted to.

The only place she could find, though, was in the back, where there was a half empty pew after a family had sat there for a while then left. She decided that she might as well slip in and vowed to be more organized next week, specifically asking someone to sit with her. Or save her a seat. Amy would have if she would have said something.

Regardless, she settled down, her Bible on her lap, her heart eager to hear and see the message that the pastor had planned. She heard they were always very good.

Just as the pianist stopped playing and the song leader stepped to the pulpit, someone slipped in beside her, and she glanced up, already moving over.

She almost froze when she saw Judd.

Of course, he would come in late, having to take care of his horses and wagon, probably giving them water, feed, and maybe loosening their lines? She wasn't sure what exactly went into taking care of horses, but she supposed that she shouldn't have been surprised.

She gave him a smile and slid over.

He sat down, and maybe it was the church, or maybe it was the good lighting, but she felt like he was much bigger today than he had been last night at supper. Which was not necessarily a bad thing. She just...felt protected. Of course, it sparked that feeling in her heart, whether it was attraction or just the way someone felt when they were with a good friend.

Or maybe it was a mix of both.

Which was completely ludicrous, since he wasn't a good friend. She'd just met him less than a week ago and she had spent exactly one meal chatting with him, and half of that conversation had been as awkward as a conversation could possibly be.

Regardless, she was pleasantly surprised as they stood singing the first hymn when his voice blended with hers, a rich tenor that made her want to sing even more from her heart. The song service was almost always her favorite part, since she loved the hymns and enjoyed harmony, but she never enjoyed it quite like she did while sitting beside Judd.

The sermon was excellent, and the service was over before she knew it. Judd had slipped out early, and she assumed it was so that he could get his horses and wagon ready to give rides to the children.

She was a little bit jealous when she saw Amy slipping out as well, which was ridiculous but maybe a little understandable. Amy was going to get to work with Judd and the kids.

And she hadn't considered it before, but Amy and Judd...they were very similar ages. Terry was just two years older than Amy, and Judd must have been very close to that since they were in the same grade. They would be perfect together. Judd enjoyed horses, and he'd been brought up on a farm, and Amy had never met an animal that she didn't love.

Terry had nothing to do with animals and only loved them because her sister did for the most part, and she wasn't nearly as good with children as Amy was—maybe she was good at keeping them well and entertaining them for a couple of minutes in an exam room, but she couldn't keep an entire wagonload of kids singing songs and playing games and enjoying a wagon ride while not fighting or trying to jump off. But Amy had kept everything together, and it was one of her strengths.

Terry knew this, but still, the idea that Amy was with Judd gave her a feeling that she didn't like. Although, whether it was the feeling she didn't like or the fact that she felt it, she wasn't sure.

Chapter Thirteen

*T*erry had made a fruit salad to take to her mom's. And she stopped by the duplex on the way there. Not being in a rush because she knew that Amy, at least, would be late since she was riding with Judd to take the kids home.

Still, she didn't mess around because she was eager to talk to her mom. That was one of the things she missed the most about being gone for the last dozen years or so, being able to just sit down and have a chat with her mother. Her mom had so much wisdom and always had such great ideas, saw things in a way that Terry often didn't, probably because of her experience in the world, and Terry loved chatting with her.

As she drove to her mom's house though, she thought that perhaps God had brought her back not just so that she could partake of her mom's wisdom again, but perhaps because her mom needed her.

She thought that again as she walked in and saw the kids playing and running around, with Gilbert in the kitchen giving their mom a hand.

It would have been a good scene, except for the knowledge that their wife and mother was in a hospital in Richmond, and Gilbert would be leaving almost as soon as dinner was over to go back to her.

That they were struggling with the idea of whether or not they should tell the children that they had almost given up hope. That their mom might never come home again.

All of those were sobering thoughts and especially hard with Thanksgiving less than a week away.

Maybe she picked a bad time to open her clinic, she thought, not for the first time. But it was the best that she could do, and she would roll with what she had. That was kind of what life was. Taking what you'd been given and making the most out of it.

"Hey! It's so nice to see you. You don't know how we've missed your presence at our Sunday dinners," her mom said, drying her hands on her apron as she came to wrap Terry in a hug.

Their dad had died of a stroke, and it had left their mom devastated. She wasn't sure that their love affair had been huge, but they'd been good friends. And while her dad was imperfect, she knew she had lucked out in the parental department.

It made her wonder what kind of parents Judd had.

She shook her head. Where had that thought come from?

"Same, Mom. You don't know how happy I am to be back. I'm so glad you're still doing these. I feel like I missed out on so much family stuff by not being able to come for so many years."

"And you have, but now you're here, and you won't be missing out anymore."

"Well, we can start out with me pulling my weight. Give me a job," she said as the door opened and Wilson came in. He must have stopped at his house to change as well. Figuring on the same thing that Amy wasn't going to be there for a while and they all knew that they wouldn't start eating until everyone was there.

Roland was a little later. He was probably the sibling that Terry knew the least well. He was the youngest, and there were eight years between them. She had graduated from high school and left while he had still been in elementary school.

She felt like she'd missed so much with her siblings, and while she didn't regret her career path, she wished there had been a way for her to have known her siblings and have somehow been able to stay.

Like they were an old-fashioned family where everyone just stayed and worked on the farm, and no one went away.

She didn't really want that, or at least she didn't think so, although she thought that it might be a little bit better way of life.

Her mom gave her a job setting the food on the table, since Amy had texted and said that she was on her way.

Terry had just finished getting everything ready and calling the kids to wash their hands when Amy and Jones walked in.

Terry smiled and threw up a hand since she was on the opposite end of the table, and the kids were running toward Amy to greet her, when she froze.

Judd walked in behind them.

Oh. Wow. So Amy had invited him to Sunday dinner? That was huge. There must be something really serious going on in their relationship. Maybe they were together and Terry hadn't even known it.

She couldn't wait to get Amy alone and ask her. She definitely had not seen this coming. Or she would have completely ignored that little buzz of attraction she felt every time she was around Judd. She probably wouldn't have had dinner with him last night, and she was grateful that she had turned down his invitation to sit by the fire, as tempting as it was. It wasn't that she had so much work to do necessarily, although she did, she just didn't want to spend too much time with him, and she thought she should listen to her instincts.

The entire family had greeted Amy and Jones, and Terry walked over to give her a hug.

Judd was still standing beside Jones and her, although Wilson had come over and shook his hand and they chatted about a few different things.

"Look what I found on the street corner, thinking he was going to eat Sunday dinner by himself?" Amy said as she pointed toward Judd.

"Stop it. You know I found him. You can't take credit for everything," Jones said as he slapped Amy's hand down and stepped in front of her. "I'm the one who invited him to Sunday dinner."

"This isn't even your family," Amy said, wrinkling up her nose.

Jones did not always act like a veterinarian, but when he and Amy were together, it was impossible to tell what in the world they were going to do. It had been that way forever. Terry smiled and rolled her eyes, and gave Jones a hug. He was like family to them. In fact, it wasn't the slightest bit surprising that he was at Sunday dinner. But Judd? That was a shock.

By the time everyone had their hands washed and they settled down, and Gilbert said grace, Terry would have thought she would have gotten herself calmed down. Except, somehow she ended up seated beside Judd.

She wasn't entirely sure how that happened, since she had been helping one of the kids and then went to turn to sit in the chair that she had chosen for herself, when she realized it was already full. So she had walked around until she came to an empty chair, and it happened to be beside Judd who just happened to have put his hand on the back of the chair beside it just as she reached for her chair.

She didn't think either one of them planned it; she knew that she didn't.

But everything was so crazy, which it often was on Sundays, that no one really had an assigned seat.

Still, she kept her hands clasped tightly in her lap as her brother prayed and tried to focus on saying her own prayer for Sally.

And ignore the man beside her.

What was he doing here?

Somehow he ended up beside her in church, and now he was

beside her at Sunday dinner, and Amy seemed to be the one he was after, yet...he kept ending up with her.

After Gilbert said amen, there was some chatter around the table as they passed all the dishes. Her mother had made fried chicken, and there was mashed potatoes and gravy as well as a few different vegetables and of course her fruit salad and coleslaw.

It was a hodgepodge of things, but it made a great meal. She hadn't planned with anyone, because fruit salad went with pretty much anything, but perhaps her mom had coordinated with Amy who had brought the mashed potatoes in a crockpot.

"Who do you think put the decorations up?" her mom asked, once they had settled down and everyone had started eating.

"That's a great question," Roland said. "I've heard that some people are going to be setting up some video cameras, trying to catch the person who did it."

"Can I stay up late and see if I can catch them?" Lucas asked eagerly. He was right at the age, twelve, where this type of thing truly appealed to him. Of course, Terry wasn't sure what age they outgrew that.

She certainly hadn't, and she was tempted to call out right away and volunteer to go with him, but Gilbert said, "No. Sorry, son. You're not going out that late on a school night."

"But this is Thanksgiving week! I'll have Thursday and Friday off!"

"If the rest of the decorations are not up by then, we'll think about it. But it's a definite no on a school night."

Terry felt bad for Gilbert. It was the kind of thing where Gilbert might have said to his son, "Sure, let's do it together." She could totally see that. But not with his wife in the hospital. Not with him spending every waking second trying to be a dad and a husband and still try to keep his equipment rental business going. He had employees who worked the office, but he was usually the face and salesman.

In fact, thinking about that, Terry wondered how it was going.

He'd been so preoccupied with his wife, she wondered if he'd even had time to take care of it.

The thought tugged at her heart and also scared her. Maybe that was why Gilbert had moved in with their mom. Because his business wasn't making any money, and his wife needed him.

Regardless, it stunk to see Lucas's downturned face.

"Well, I for one am just going to let them be. Whoever it is obviously doesn't want a bunch of attention drawn to them, and I'm going to respect that," Wilson said, although he added with a cheeky grin, "However, if I get up in the middle of the night and feel like taking a drive, and happen to drive down Main Street, well, so be it."

Everyone around the table laughed.

"It's actually my job to chronicle that now," Terry offered, knowing that it was probably going to elicit groans.

She was not wrong. The entire table erupted, even the children getting into it, although she didn't think they knew what for.

"Mrs. Tucker caught you! I'm so sorry I wasn't there to run interference."

"You can't protect me from everything," Terry said, smiling at Amy and appreciating the thought. The idea that she would make sure that her big sister was protected, when it used to be the other way around.

But that just seemed to be Amy, always trying to take care of things.

"Yes. But yes, Mrs. Tucker caught me. And now I have all the information to make social media posts for the town."

"That's cool. So how much are you going to sell it to me for?" Roland asked with a gleam in his eye.

"I don't trust that look. I think it's probably more than you can afford."

Roland grinned, like he knew that he probably couldn't afford whatever she was going to ask.

It felt so good to be back with the family.

"Did you hear that Mrs. Rosario has a squirrel in her house?" her mom asked, after the table fell silent.

"What? A squirrel?" Gilbert said, his head popping up. It was probably nice to try to get his mind off thinking about his wife, with something as benign and crazy as that.

"Yeah. Apparently she's not sure how it got in, but she's tried to leave the door open and chase it out, and it just runs right by the open door. Doesn't have anything to do with it."

"She should leave a trail of nuts for it," Roland said.

"She's done that too. Apparently, it would rather eat the granola on her kitchen counter than the nuts she leaves as a trail to go out the door."

"You better watch that she doesn't accidentally allow a bunch of other things in that she doesn't want while she's trying to get the squirrel out," Amy said, and Terry had to agree.

"I think she even has a trap for it," their mom said, hurrying to add, "The kind that doesn't kill them, but just traps them inside? Like you might catch a feral cat to take it to the vet to get it fixed and shots."

"I've seen those kinds of traps lots of times. In fact, if she needs any, I have a few in the storage shed outside my practice," Jones offered, sounding much more like a veterinarian there than he had when he was talking with Amy.

She thought that they had been slapping each other under the table earlier, but she couldn't be sure. Probably because Amy thought that Jones was like one centimeter on her side or something.

Terry didn't roll her eyes, but she felt like it.

"What is she going to do?" Terry asked, glad that it wasn't her, although her landlord should take care of those kinds of things for her. Her landlord, who had been conspicuously quiet during the entire meal so far.

She tried to glance over at him, but she was afraid that he would see her looking at him and glance over at her, and then she'd be caught awkwardly looking at him for no reason. So she just kept her eyes on her plate after she asked her question.

"She's not sure. She doesn't want to call an exterminator, because she's afraid that they'll kill the squirrel. Plus, she doesn't have a whole lot of money."

Their mom's voice dropped on that last note, and the table was quiet for just a moment. Mrs. Rosario was well loved in the community, and she'd been a teacher for a number of years. She had a good pension and Social Security, but a lot of that was going to help keep her husband in a memory care facility. He'd had Alzheimer's for years, and she had no longer been able to care for him. She visited him on a daily basis, most of the time going and staying all day.

"This gives her something to do. Something to take her mind off everything else that's going on," Gilbert said.

Terry figured she knew where that came from, and she couldn't disagree.

"I can go help with the squirrel!" Lucas said, and Terry couldn't help but think how sweet and adorable he was. He was probably just dying for something to do, for someone to spend time with him.

"I heard some people at church giving her some advice, and maybe she'll get it taken care of. It can't stay in her house forever."

"Well, it's getting food, and I assume it can probably drink out of the toilet. Do squirrels drink?" Roland asked the table at large, but no one knew the answer to that.

"Aren't you the animal expert?" Roland asked, looking at Jones.

"Well, I do small animals and occasionally large animals, but I have to admit, I've never had a squirrel. And I don't think I had a single class about squirrels in my entire academic career. So, yes, but no," he said. "But," he elbowed Amy, "Amy takes all kinds, so maybe you should ask her, since she seems to be the local animal expert far above and beyond me."

Amy rolled her eyes. "Stop it, already. You're the one with doctor in front of your name."

"You're the one with the whole compound full of animals."

"There's nothing wrong with that."

"I didn't say there was, unless you happen to be your best friend, who gets roped into helping you every time you need help with them."

Jones didn't add "and you can't afford to pay them," but Terry kind of did that in her head. She wanted to talk to her about it more but hadn't had a chance. The Sunday dinner table hardly seemed like the place.

"Regardless, I've heard that squirrels, while not aggressive, can really give a terrible bite."

"I've heard that too," Terry said.

"I treated a dog that was attacked by a rabid squirrel once, and it looked worse than a lot of those I've seen that have been in a dogfight," Jones volunteered.

They talked about it for a bit more, and then their mom said, "Are we going to eat here for Thanksgiving? I guess I should have planned things earlier, but everything has been a little unstable, with Gilbert moving in and Terry moving back and all of the crazy things that have been happening."

It was probably about having a whole bunch of people in her house, and trying to figure out what to do for Gilbert and his wife, and that type of thing.

"I'm happy to cook or help whoever else is doing it. I can be here all day. The clinic was already planning on being closed on Thursday, although we open back up on Friday." Terry spoke up, eager to jump into the holiday preparations.

"After I'm done with the animals in the morning, I can come give you a hand as well."

"We don't have school, and I can help!" Lucas said.

Gilbert was conspicuously silent, and Terry figured that meant that he had no idea what he'd be doing on Thursday. Or what his wife would be like.

"I have some leaf blowing to do in the morning, and... I was looking for some help with that," Judd began.

"I can! I can help. I'm good at that. I helped Dad do it last year, although we haven't done it this year yet," Lucas said, his voice trailing off a bit.

"Wow, would you really help? I was hoping for someone with your kind of enthusiasm and experience," Judd said, and Terry wanted to reach over and hug him. It was so obvious that Lucas was dying for attention, and scared, and wanted to do something, have a job, a purpose. And she just wanted to hug him too. But Judd had seen that and thought of something that he could do to help.

"Actually, maybe we could even blow the leaves around your grandma's house, just for practice, before we go to the job that I have to do."

"You think so?" Lucas asked, looking first at Judd and then at his gram. "Could I?"

"Well, if your dad says it's okay, and Judd's sure he wants you, I'd love to have my leaves blown. I just haven't gotten around to that this year yet."

He looked at his dad, who didn't say anything. Terry thought that she would probably be a terrible mother, because all he had to do was look at her with those big eyes and she would have let him do anything.

Gilbert finally nodded. And he gave a grateful look at Judd before he looked again at his son. "But I want to hear that you're good help and not that you were messing around, okay?"

"I'm a good worker, Dad. And I'll do a really great job."

"I might be able to pay you a little bit of something, but we'll have to see how the job goes, okay?" Judd said, and Terry wanted to slip him money under the table immediately. He just did odd jobs around the town and didn't earn much at all, and yet there he was, offering to pay her nephew and making his eyes light up so bright. What a kind thing to do for a kid who was losing his mom and maybe didn't even understand what was happening. Although, at Lucas's age, he probably did. Maybe he just didn't want to face it.

But the tone of the table had changed somewhat, and Terry was pretty sure her entire family appreciated what Judd had just done. Gilbert most of all. In fact, if she didn't know him better, she'd almost say that Gilbert was tearing up.

He must feel pulled in so many different directions, like he couldn't be a good husband if he wasn't with his wife, but he couldn't be a good father if he wasn't with his kids, and then he had to try to make a living and support everyone because that was his job as a Christian dad, to provide, and...she'd always seen it from the other end. From the person in the hospital, treating them, in residency, where she'd look at them, and she hadn't realized all the things that had been going on behind the scenes. Because while not everyone had children, things were always complicated by medical conditions.

She tucked that thought away, hoping to be more compassionate to the patients she served in this town. She didn't intend to have anything to do with hospitals, but everyone had trials that they were facing, and kindness and empathy, and giving a helping hand like Judd had just showed, went a long way.

"While I'm thinking about it, Judd," her mother started. "You were included in that invitation to Thanksgiving, although we didn't say specifically."

"With the McBrides, you just got to show up, and they feed you. You don't even have to really know them," Jones said, and everyone around the table laughed, because Jones had been doing that for years. Although of course, Amy was his best friend, and he was almost a part of the family.

Terry looked at them elbowing each other, like kids or...like people who liked each other for more than friends.

The idea was new, since she hadn't really thought about it, but maybe as she came back, looking at everything with new eyes, she was seeing something that she hadn't seen before. Her sister, and the idea that she and Jones might be perfect for each other.

In fact, as she was watching, Jones gave Amy a look when she wasn't looking that made Terry think that she was exactly right, even if the two of them didn't know it.

"Well, thanks, but I'll probably be with my parents," Judd said.

"We usually have our meal early, so if you're able, you're welcome."

"We'll see. Usually they have theirs later, so maybe. Thanks so much, I appreciate it."

Terry looked at Judd fully for the first time since they'd sat down. She found him already staring at her.

She wasn't quite sure what was in his gaze, but she gave him a smile, mostly because she appreciated what he was doing with Lucas, but also just because she wanted to, and she couldn't quite understand why.

The thought of Amy came into her head, and she looked away quickly. Not wanting to get between the two of them. Just in case she was wrong about Jones and Amy, which she very well could be. She was hardly a romantic.

Chapter Fourteen

"That was delicious. Thank you so much everyone who brought something, and if you couldn't, don't feel bad. You can see there's plenty left over," Mrs. McBride said as she stood from the table. The kids had long since been excused, and they'd all had some fruit salad and chocolate cake for dessert. There were several steaming cups of coffee still sitting on the table, and everyone seemed reluctant to get up and leave. Perhaps it was because everyone felt like taking a nap, or maybe they were like Judd, who just enjoyed the camaraderie. He had been an only child, and his dinnertimes had been nothing like the McBrides' table.

He had enjoyed every second, even though he was introverted and didn't really enjoy interacting with people on a regular basis. Still, seeing the way everyone felt at ease with each other, obviously loving each other and wanting the best for them, while still not being afraid to tease and pick on each other, had been priceless.

"I can give you a hand cleaning up, Mom," Terry said immediately as she stood.

It had made the dinner a little bit awkward since he'd been stuck beside Terry. Not exactly stuck, but...she always made him, not nervous, just aware. Very aware of her. Plus, add that to the fact that he admired her for wanting to return home to her hometown and giving up what probably could have been a very lucrative career in a bigger practice.

She seemed very content and happy to be home with her family, helping.

He hadn't missed a grateful look that she'd shot him when he offered to have Lucas help him blow leaves.

Sometimes he didn't understand why other people didn't think of the things that he did. But he'd just started to understand that it was one of the things that he was good at. He didn't have a big name anywhere and wasn't super intelligent or talented about anything, except seeing people and their needs and knowing what needed to be done to meet those needs.

"Terry, would you mind taking Judd home with you? Jones and I were going to stay here for a bit and play with the kids."

"Of course not," Terry said, looking up, surprise flashing across her face before she smiled.

"Thanks. Judd, you don't mind, do you?"

"I appreciate the ride, although she doesn't have to if she doesn't want to." He waited until Terry met his gaze. "Although we are going to the same place."

"Of course. I don't mind at all as long as you don't mind waiting a little bit. I want to give my mom a hand cleaning up before I run out."

"I can help too," he said easily, starting to clear plates off the table. Lucas must have been watching him from across the room, because as soon as he saw Judd starting to clean off the table, he came over and started to give a hand as well.

"I can see you're a worker," Judd said, ruffling the boy's hair, which made him beam.

"I like to work," Lucas said, and Judd bit back a smile. He probably liked to work until he got tired of it, like every other kid on the planet, but he didn't say anything. It took a lot of self-control and maturity before a person could push themselves to do things that they really didn't want to do. Although, Lucas was at the age where he could start learning those things.

"If you're sending leftovers, I'll take a couple of pieces of chocolate cake, or the whole thing or whatever," Roland said as he carried dishes to the island in the middle of the kitchen for them to be scooped into containers. They always sent the leftovers to whatever home they could.

"You're welcome to take it all if you want to. I actually made two, because I figured I would want another one for the kids this week. I'll be busy making pies and getting things ready for the Thanksgiving meal, and I won't have a lot of time to make goodies."

"All right. I'm not going to argue with that," Roland said, dropping a kiss on his mom's cheek and throwing up a hand that encompassed the rest of the room. "I need to get going. It's good to see you all. See you on Thursday,"

It was interesting that Mrs. McBride had six kids, and only two of them were married. He supposed modern people were waiting to get married until they were older, and he couldn't fault anyone for that since he had done the same thing.

"Did you give Roland all the cake again?" Wilson asked as he came out from where he had been playing with the children in the living room.

"I'm sorry, I didn't realize you wanted some," Mrs. McBride said, stopping and looking at her son like she had forgotten he existed. She probably had a lot on her mind.

"I can't believe it. Betrayed by my own mother."

"If you run, you could probably catch him," Terry said. "Although, you might have to wrestle him in order to get him to share the cake. He was pretty quick to grab it and take off."

"I'll catch him," Wilson said as he hurried out the door.

Judd somehow found himself standing at the sink, rinsing dishes off and stacking them in the dishwasher. He listened to the chatter that was going on behind him between Terry and her mom and

Marissa, Gilbert's middle child, and the one who seemed to be the most lost. The boys were acting like boys, while Marissa was quiet and subdued, maybe missing their mom.

Regardless, she'd come out and sat down at the counter, eating a cookie even though they just had a meal, with the dog who had been playing with the kids coming out and lying at her feet. Judd didn't understand how she could eat another thing, except maybe she hadn't eaten as much as he had. He hadn't noticed. He felt like someone should be watching her specially, but the ladies probably had it covered.

As he finished rinsing the dishes and put the last one in the dishwasher, Terry came over to the sink, shaking the rag out and rinsing it, the way she had when they had cooked dinner the night before.

He looked over at her. Maybe she was having the same memories, because their eyes met and it was like something passed between them.

"I appreciate you two sticking around and helping me with the cleanup," Mrs. McBride said, and he jerked his gaze away from Terry's. He wasn't quite sure what was going on there, but he just wanted to keep looking at her.

"No problem, ma'am," he said.

"Any time, Mom. I feel like I have a lot of making up to do for the times I wasn't here."

"Don't worry about it. Sally was always a lot of help, and I know Gilbert is preoccupied, or Amy would be out here helping us rather than playing with the kids."

"I think we're going to head out," Terry said, looking at Judd with questions in her eyes.

He nodded. It was her family; he didn't need to stay any longer.

"I think I'm going to get going too," Gilbert said, coming into the kitchen with a bag thrown over his shoulder. "I'm not sure how soon I'll be home," he said, sighing. "I hate to throw all of this on you, Mom."

"Don't you worry about a thing. I've raised kids before, and I certainly know what to do with them. Three is easy. It's when you have six that it gets hard."

They all chuckled a little, but having Gilbert in the room felt like getting splashed in the face with cold water. And he wasn't sure what to do about it.

"Thanks, Mom," Terry said, hugging her mom and following Judd out the door.

It had barely closed behind them when she sighed and said, "I wish there was more that we can do for Gilbert, but I really, really appreciate what you did with Lucas. You made his day, and I thought Gilbert was going to cry right there at the table."

He figured being away from her family had been hard, and coming back, seeing all the problems, that life wasn't just peachy, had made it even worse for her. Like she'd missed out, and maybe she could have helped more, maybe in Gilbert's situation, and seeing that her mom had a heavy burden. And then those children. How could her heart not bleed for the children?

"I'm happy to do it. The leaves need to be blown anyway. I noticed that as I was walking in, and I kinda figured I would offer to do it, but with Lucas wanting to help so much, it was perfect."

"Yeah, I don't know how much help he'll be, but I know he'll appreciate the attention."

"I'll try to make sure he enjoys it. Work doesn't have to be drudgery all the time."

"Sometimes you just have to suck it up and do it, but sometimes if you have the right attitude, it makes everything a lot easier."

He looked at her, agreeing. But surprised. Most people thought of their job as something that they had to get through in order to be able to play on the weekends or in the evening or whatever, but he'd always figured that it was a smarter idea to just enjoy what he did, since he spent so much time on it.

It almost sounded like Terry had the exact same idea, and he wanted to talk to her about it, but he figured that he better hold his peace. He'd already met her eyes several times, and each time, he felt that tug inside and had trouble pulling his eyes away. He didn't want her to notice.

They walked to her car, and he debated with himself for about three seconds before he walked to the driver side and opened the door for her.

She seemed extremely surprised. "Thank you. I wasn't expecting that."

"I'm sorry. I debated about whether or not to do it, but it just seemed like the right thing to do." He wasn't sure that he would have opened it for anyone else, and he hadn't opened it for Amy when she offered to give him a ride home from the animal sanctuary where they'd dropped off the horses. Of course, Jones was talking to her, and he couldn't even remember where she was when he got in the car. But he couldn't forget where Terry was, which was new. He didn't typically have that kind of bead on people, a woman, especially. He didn't like it but didn't know how to get himself to stop.

They didn't talk much on the way home. Maybe Terry felt the same way he did—like he needed a nap. Whatever it was, she parked, and they got out, walking silently up the sidewalk of the duplex to the front door.

"What are your plans for this afternoon?" Terry asked, almost as though she belatedly realized that maybe she should have been making conversation.

"Probably take a nap," he said. Although it was what he wanted to do, it wasn't what he was most likely going to do. "You?"

"I thought the same. Although, I also thought I might take a walk to the clinic. I am eager for tomorrow, but also nervous."

"I don't know why you're nervous. Dr. Vivik had a fabulous practice, and the people in town love you. You're going to be great."

He didn't know why he felt like he needed to encourage her, but he did.

"Thanks," she said as he opened the door for her and she walked in. She started toward the stairs, while he stood at the bottom. Wanting to wait until she got upstairs before he started what he was planning on doing.

She realized he wasn't following her and turned. "I guess I'll see you later, maybe."

"Yeah. Have a nice nap," he said, unsure if that was what she was going to do. He turned, walking into his living room.

It was sparse, with just a recliner which he loved and a sofa which he slept on at times. It was comfortable, well-worn and serviceable, but not aesthetically pleasing. He hadn't picked out any of the things in his house for their looks. That was...the job of the wife, he supposed, although he hadn't thought a lot about having one.

He pulled out his phone, sat down on his recliner, and dialed his parents' number for his weekly requisite call to them.

"Hello." It was his dad who answered. He'd called his mom.

"Hey, Dad. How are you?"

"Doing good. Business is up, stocks are up, and the NASDAQ is soaring. I couldn't ask for better times, unless I had a son who was interested in taking over the reins of the business."

"Sounds good. I'm glad everything's going so well for you." He never knew what to say to his dad. He was a businessman and had wanted Judd to follow in his footsteps. Judd hadn't been the slightest bit interested, although when his great-uncle had died and left his fortune to Judd, Judd had tried to invest it wisely and had made some good decisions with his dad's help. He didn't hate his dad. They just didn't always see things eye to eye, which he figured was probably common. It made him sad, because he would like to have had a better relationship with him, but they just didn't.

"Your mom's here. Want to talk to her?"

"Sure," he said. Knowing that he didn't have a whole lot more to say to his mom. She lived in the high-society life, which she loved. Although, she also loved spending time on the farm that was about halfway up Mistletoe Mountain. They raised high-dollar horses, and occasionally she rescued some, although she didn't take care of them herself. They hired people to do that, of course.

He'd grown up there, running wild through the fields, playing in the creek, and back when his dad had run a few beef cattle, he had helped with that and the horses.

The beef cattle were long gone, and the horses almost exclusively taken care of by hired help now.

"Hello, Judson," his mom said, and he smiled, because she always used his full name. Most people didn't even know he had a name other than Judd. Leave it to his mom to always remember. Of course, she named him, and she must be partial to it.

"Hey, Mom. What's up?"

"Well, I have a son who hasn't been home in more than a month. And I don't know whether he's coming home for Thanksgiving or not. I don't know how I would find out about that."

He wanted to say, "maybe you could call him and ask," but he didn't. If he wanted to talk to his parents, he called them.

"Where are you having Thanksgiving?" he asked, wishing that he would be able to make it to the McBride Thanksgiving, although while he believed that they didn't mind him going, it was a family holiday, and he wasn't family.

"We're going to have it on the farm. I will have a few extra people there. The state transportation secretary and a close friend of his and their wives will be with us. It will be formal, so be sure to wear a tie."

"Got it," he said, groaning in his soul. He had one suit and tie that he kept for that very reason—any time he was called to go to dinner at his parents' house.

It was the only time he wore it. He didn't even wear it to church. He hadn't even worn it to the last funeral that he'd gone to. And he'd noticed that he wasn't the only one who didn't wear them.

Some of the older folk had them on, but the trend was toward a more casual way of dressing. He welcomed that trend.

"Is there anything I can bring?" he asked, which he did every time, and of course his mother would decline.

"No, Patty has it all under control. If she needs anything, she goes to the grocery store and gets it. Although, for goodness' sake, I don't want her buying any more of those cheap olives. They were so disgusting last time."

Judd remembered his mom complaining about the olives, but he hadn't noticed a difference in taste himself. Most likely, she hadn't either but had seen an off-brand jar in her kitchen, which was guaranteed to set her off.

"I can bring some fancy olives if you want me to," he offered, knowing she would decline.

"Judd, just get yourself a wife or, at the very least, a girlfriend. You are interested in girls, correct?"

He closed his eyes. This was a conversation that they had a good bit. He had never brought a girl home, and it bothered his mother to no end. He just hadn't met anyone who he was interested in. He had a tendency to see the world through the lens of people he could help and not people he could hook up with.

Terry's face came into his mind, and he bit back a sigh. She was someone he could see himself taking to his parents' house, although she would hate it. But he could see himself with her. Not hooking up, unless the hookup lasted a lifetime. That was the only kind he was interested in.

He never knew how to answer his mom, though. So he just stayed silent.

"Sometimes you scare me, Judd," his mother said. Then she sighed again. "If you bring a man home, at least don't make it one of those scruffy, feminist, you can't tell whether it's a boy or girl kind of thing," his mother said, and he could just see her putting her hand on her forehead and acting put out.

"You don't need to worry about that, Mom," he said. They didn't know him at all if they thought he would do that, and that was kind of the story between him and his parents. They didn't know him at all.

He could lay the blame at their feet, but it was his fault as well.

He just wasn't interested in their lifestyle. Not even a little. But this phone call was his attempt to be a dutiful son. If he didn't make it, he would go months without hearing from them. Once, he hadn't heard from them for an entire year, until the next holiday season had rolled around and his mother had called angrily demanding why he hadn't gone to Thanksgiving dinner.

He hadn't gone because he hadn't been invited.

And she informed him that he hadn't been invited because he hadn't called her for her to be able to invite him. It was like she didn't know how to use her telephone.

"You know, I'm not getting any younger, and you could make me very happy. I don't know why you refuse to do that. It's like making me happy hurts you in some kind of weird way," his mother said in the tone that made him feel like he was about half an inch tall.

"Someday, Mom."

"Have you done anything constructive with your life?"

He knew that by constructive she meant had he gone to college yet. That was the only thing that she deemed constructive. And the fact that he hadn't gone irritated her to no end. He had no desire to go, no need. He didn't want to have a job that needed a college education, and he wasn't going to waste his money just so he could get a diploma and say he went. That was ridiculous.

Plus, he had things that were going on here, and he wasn't going to leave them.

"Well, it's been nice talking to you. I'll talk to you again next Sunday," he said, feeling a sinking feeling in his soul, a bit of emptiness there that he knew could be better, but he didn't know how. When one's parents didn't really seem to like one, there just wasn't anything a person could do about it.

Lord, I've always tried to show them You, but they never seem to see it.

He always thought about that verse, it was easier for a camel to go through the eye of a needle than for a rich man to enter into heaven. He could kind of understand it. His parents didn't need or want for anything, they had no need for God, and they didn't understand why he did.

Maybe that was why he had eschewed the wealth and had chosen a simple lifestyle, one that was humble and sought to serve others. He just wanted to live what he read in the Bible.

That was all.

They hung up, and he sat there for a little bit, holding his phone in his hand and wondering if, by some miracle, he ever did get married, whether he would know how to actually raise a good family or not. He had no experience in that. Other than what he'd seen in other people's families, like the McBrides today.

He waited until he thought that Terry was probably asleep. Then, he shoved his phone in his pocket, grabbed his coat from where he had laid it on the chair, shoved his hands in, and quietly walked out of the living room and out of his house. He had a squirrel to catch.

Chapter Fifteen

*J*udd must have taken one hen of a nap, Terry thought to herself as she stood in the kitchen, trying to figure out whether she should eat supper by herself or wait a little longer. It was six o'clock on the dot, and in her experience, sometimes people said six o'clock but they meant nine.

Judd wasn't like that, she knew, but... Still, as the clock clicked to 6:01, she tried to figure out what to do.

She could sit at the table and make a list of the things that she wanted to be sure to tell each of her patients. She'd already made a document that she had instructed her secretary to email to each of her patients.

She had all of her payment channels set up, and her bank account had been switched. She thought she was ready. Hoped she was.

She heard a noise at the door and then the doorknob rattling, as though someone were trying to get in but couldn't quite grab a hold of it.

She glanced at the clock.

6:03.

What in the world? This was one of those times where she wished she had a dog. Something that wasn't ferocious exactly, but that would give someone a second thought before they came barging into her house. Except, it wasn't her house, and she couldn't deny that relief flooded her soul as the familiar figure of Judd came walking through the door.

Except, it looked like there was some kind of bandage on his hand.

It was bright red.

Her hand went to her throat, and she jumped up and hurried forward.

"What in the world?" she said as he closed the door behind him and looked at her, and if she wasn't mistaken, his look said he wished that she hadn't seen him.

"Nothing," he said, pushing off the door and turning toward his side of the duplex, his hand out to reach for the doorknob.

"We're not eating supper?" she asked, coming a little closer and wondering if he was drunk. He seemed...unsteady.

"Oh. I forgot about supper."

Were there bars open on Sunday?

She knew there were. The idea of bars being closed on Sundays had ended a long time ago even though her parents had always taught them that Sunday was a special day set aside for the Lord, where a person was supposed to try to rest, despite the fact that they were no longer under the Sabbath laws.

"I have it ready, but I don't want to force you to eat. I was just kind of waiting on you, because I didn't want to eat without you."

"I should have given you my number," he said, almost as though he were thinking out loud.

"Yeah. That would be nice. I would have texted you, and then...if you already ate, it wouldn't have been a big deal."

"I haven't," he said.

He had kinda shoved his hand behind him, not exactly holding it like he was guilty of something, but he had shifted his body so that it was between her and his hand.

"Did you cut your hand?"

"No," he said.

"But that bandage has blood on it, right?" She was a doctor, she ought to know what blood looked like. She'd seen more than her share of dirty bandages.

"Yes. It does."

"So let me look at it," she said.

He didn't say anything, just stood there.

"You know I'm a doctor, right?"

He gave her a baleful look.

"Come to the kitchen. Whatever is going on, it's fine. You're not going to shock me. I'm not going to faint at the sight of blood."

"I do," he said, leaning against the door and looking at her with eyes that seemed to be held open by sheer willpower.

"Oh." That was his problem. "Well, come on. Let's go to the table, and I'll get you fixed up. You don't have to look."

He pursed his lips, and then he said, "This sounds terrible, but I'm not sure I can make it."

"You made it to the house somehow, unless you just cut it outside, and that's interesting and a little scary that you carry bandages around in your pocket."

"No. I told myself if I made it to the house, that was as far as I had to go."

"Fine. Sit down right there, we'll get as much light on it as we can, and we'll figure it out."

One eye seemed to drift shut, and he looked at her as though she had grown two heads, possibly because he was dizzy and it looked like she had.

"Go to the kitchen," he said, not looking happy about it, his lips pulled back.

"Let me help you," she said, slipping her hand around his waist and standing beside his good hand, in case he wanted to put it on her shoulder and allow her to help him.

He did, which she was grateful for. He seemed very woozy. She knew that some people really did pass out or get sick at the sight of blood. She knew several people from college who had planned to be doctors but at the first sight of blood had realized that it was going to be impossible. And had to change their majors.

Thankfully, that wasn't her.

They awkwardly shuffled down the hall, with him putting a hand and elbow out and her touching the wall for balance.

He was heavy and big. She already knew that, but she'd not been this close to him before, and...she kind of liked it.

Always before, she'd been able to keep a professional distance from anyone she'd treated, but she knew before they even made it to the kitchen that Judd was different.

Grabbing a chair with her toe, she pulled on it carefully but quickly, making sure it didn't tilt over as she moved it from the table and helped him to sit down.

"All right, if you don't mind, I'm going to need to unwind this bandage to see what we're dealing with." She touched the bandage, and he winced, as though it hurt, although she knew it couldn't have. So she wasn't sure exactly what the issue was. Other than he must not want her to work on him. "I need to go get my bag." She had a bag that she always kept at home for emergencies. It had novocaine in it, as well as sutures, and other things she thought she might need for an emergency like this. She could fix herself up. It was one of the benefits of being a doctor.

He jerked his head but didn't say anything, and she left, hurrying up to her room to grab her bag.

What in the world could he have done that would have caused him to bleed like that but not be cut? Had he been attacked? She wasn't sure, but hopefully now that he was sitting down, she could find out.

Chapter Sixteen

*J*udd hadn't meant for Terry to see him. How was he going to explain that he got bitten by a squirrel? She would be suspicious immediately that he had been the one to go get the squirrel out of Mrs. Rosario's house.

He had not been the only one with the idea though, and her grandson had been there, only he was a hothead and had insisted that they were going to have to kill the squirrel.

Mrs. Rosario had pleaded with him not to, and Judd quietly tried to get the squirrel out before Jack could succeed in his mission.

Unfortunately, Jack had gotten the squirrel cornered, as he held a frying pan in his hand, intending to brain the squirrel.

Judd had grabbed a hold of his hand to keep the frying pan from coming down, but the squirrel had felt threatened enough that he had attacked both men. Jack had enough presence of mind to drop the frying pan and run. Judd had been focused on one mission, and that was to get the squirrel out of the house, so he'd run, with the squirrel biting and scratching at his hand, for the open front door. He'd been able to get out and, with a bit of effort, had been able to get the squirrel off his hand without hurting it. It had run up the nearest tree and squawked angrily from the highest branch.

Jack had been very quick to say "I told you so," and Mrs. Rosario had been very apologetic and got some bandages to give to him.

Judd, knowing he was not good with blood, had left as soon as possible and kept his hand in his lap in his car, putting pressure on it with the bandages to try to stanch the bleeding. He had done it without looking at his hand, hoping that he was doing the right thing, but unsure, not wanting to pass out while he drove.

"Would you like a drink of water or something before I get started?" Terry came back in the room, all business, carrying a bag that she set on the table and opened up.

"I'm fine," he said, wishing he felt better, because then he would have gone in his side of the duplex, where he didn't think that she would follow him.

He could be wrong though. She seemed pretty determined to take care of his hand.

Still, this whole blood thing might be a good excuse for him not to answer her questions, because he was almost one-hundred-percent sure she was going to have questions.

"How did this happen?" she asked as she snapped on a pair of gloves.

He rolled his head, and then leaving his bandaged hand in his lap, he put his other elbow on the table and put his head in his hand.

He hoped that that showed her that he was not answering her questions.

"Do you mind if I take this off?" she said, indicating the bandage.

"Go ahead. I'll look away," he said, not wanting to face the fact that he was breathless and truly was fighting to stay seated in his chair. He shouldn't have glanced down at his lap.

He closed his eyes so he wouldn't accidentally see something he didn't want to. He didn't know why blood affected him this way, but it always had. He felt a little bit like a baby, but right now, his main focus was not falling off the chair, and not passing out if possible.

"There is so much blood," she said. "Is this a cut?"

"No," he said shortly.

"All right. You answer yes or no questions. Is it from an accident?"

It was kind of an accident, but he said, "No."

"Were you in a fight?"

Technically, it was a fight with a squirrel, but he felt like the accurate answer to that question would be, "No."

"Wow. You got some jagged marks on here. This looks like a bite. You had an animal biting you." He cracked an eye to see she studied his hand, where blood still seeped from the biggest wound which was on his wrist.

"This wound is where people cut themselves if they're trying to commit suicide. But if you used a knife, at least a sharp one, it should have been straight across. This is definitely a bite. You got bitten by an animal?" She spoke as she turned his hand over from side to side, probing a little bit before he heard her bag rustle and then a chair scraping on the floor as she pulled it over, presumably to sit down on.

"Yes."

"Yeah. Definitely looks like a bite. I hope you don't mind if I sit down. If you were on a gurney, I could shift it up or down to make it so that I'm not hurting my back while I'm bending over."

"It's fine," he said. He didn't care if she lay on the floor while she took care of it. He did appreciate her taking care of it though.

"You are going to need a tetanus shot."

"Okay," he said.

"I have some at the clinic. You can come in anytime this week before four, okay?"

"Yeah," he said.

Her hand was gentle as it held his. Then, she set his hand in her lap on what felt like a towel.

He didn't watch, he couldn't, but he focused instead on the

feeling of her fingers, cool and careful, touching over his sensitive skin.

Her bag rustled again, and he cracked his eyes in time to see her reach into it and set out a few things on the table. She took a swab of cotton and poured some liquid on it.

"This might sting, but it's an antiseptic that will kill any germs."

"Good," he said. He could take the pain, didn't mind that at all. It was the blood he couldn't handle.

"I'm going to work kind of quickly, because I really want to get this one big cut stitched up. It's still seeping, although not gushing, so there's no danger. It's just once I get that done, we should be able to get the blood cleaned up, and you should be okay. You... Will you be okay once you can't see blood anymore?"

"I should be," he said, thinking back. It had been a while since he'd seen a lot of blood, and usually he was able to handle it and just have a few woozy moments. He didn't think he'd ever had something that had as much blood as this.

"All right. That's the plan then. I'll dress these other wounds once I have the big one sewn up. I am going to give you a shot of novocaine, which will numb the area, but it's probably going to sting a little. I thought I had some numbing agent in my bag, but I don't."

"Fine. I can handle the pain."

"I know you can, but I don't want to hurt you any more than what I have to. I feel a little sympathetic for you because you look so miserable right now."

"I feel miserable," he said, careful not to start talking too much. He didn't want her to get the idea that she could start asking him questions.

And indeed, while she filled the syringe and pushed the needle into his hand, she said, "What kind of animal did this to you? Was it a dog?"

"No." He racked his brain for something he could say. Something to tell her what happened without saying the exact situation. "Some dude was going to kill a squirrel, and I confronted him, and the squirrel attacked us. I...had my hand out front, because I was grabbing his weapon, and the squirrel just latched on. It must have ripped my wrist when I shook it off." There. He didn't mention that the weapon was a skillet, and he didn't mention any names, because as soon as he said Mrs. Rosario's name, she was going to remember the conversation at dinner.

"Goodness. Seems like there's a lot of outlaw squirrels running around. First Mrs. Rosario, and now you."

"Except, I prefer that my incident not get talked about in church," he said, because there were people who would pick up on that. Plus, he was talking to the person who posted about the Secret Saint and his benevolence. He didn't want any more of that than necessary, and Mrs. Rosario had promised not to tell anyone. Of course, he didn't know what her grandson was going to say.

Probably nothing good, which was just fine with Judd.

"I guess I'll have to start carrying nuts in my pocket, or granola, since that seems to be what squirrels enjoy," Judd said, hoping to move the conversation along and guide it away from any more details.

"That sounds like a good idea. In your line of work, you probably do run into squirrels. I've heard they have a tendency to build nests in houses in places where you don't want them."

She seemed like she was talking just to keep up the chatter.

"I do see a lot of squirrels," he said, to emphasize the fact that this was just another run-of-the-mill thing for him on his job.

"I didn't know they could be so ferocious," Terry said as she threaded a curved needle.

He looked away from it and closed his eyes again. Needles didn't really bother him, but he wasn't feeling the greatest, and just in case, he thought he would be better safe than sorry.

"You don't look like the kind of person who would get so woozy over blood. You know?" she said, chuckling to herself a little bit.

"Are you laughing at me?" he said without opening his eyes. He didn't care, he was just happy they weren't talking about squirrels and what happened anymore.

"Well, chuckling a little bit. After all, you do look like a tough guy."

Much to his mother's dismay. She wanted him to look like a businessman.

But that wasn't what he wanted. And while he had never been outright rebellious with his parents, he hadn't allowed them to dictate to him what he had to do.

He did value their advice and insights. And hoped that his children would do the same with him. If he ever had any.

"Does this hurt?" she asked, and he didn't feel a thing except for a little tug.

He wasn't sure exactly what she was doing, since he didn't look, but he said, "No."

"All right. You're going to feel a little bit of tugging as I stitch this up. Just let me know if you feel any pinching, which probably means I didn't get you numbed well enough. I'll give you some more."

"Nice. More drugs. That sounds good."

"No. You are not taking advantage of having a doctor as a tenant. No unnecessary drugs."

"Wow. She's strict," he said, smiling but still keeping his eyes closed. She might have stopped the bleeding, but he didn't want to take any chances.

It was a few minutes later that she said, "All right. If you can handle looking at a cut that is not bleeding, you can open your eyes. I'm going to finish cleaning the rest of this. None of the other ones are deep enough to need stitches, but I'll put a Band-Aid over this one and maybe this one here."

She touched his hand as she spoke, and he opened his eyes enough to see where her fingernail, blunt and carefully clipped short, pointed to two bigger cuts on his hand.

"You just want to be careful that you don't get these dirty. And you generally don't want to get them wet. If you don't have any gloves, I probably have some at the clinic, since Dr. Vivik had pretty big hands and he left all his supplies there. I ordered in small gloves that fit me, and that's all I have in my bag."

"I can grab some. First thing tomorrow morning or something like that. It won't be a big deal."

"All right. I just didn't know if you had work to do tonight or not. But just take it easy on that hand. Don't be using it for anything that you don't absolutely have to."

He thought about what he had been planning on doing tonight and decided that maybe he'd better text Wilson and let him know that they were going to have to take a couple days off. He hated that they weren't going to have all the Christmas decorations up, but if he gave it a few days, maybe they could do it the morning of Thanksgiving.

Of course, texting was going to be a little bit harder, as the bandage that she put on his hand inhibited the movement of his thumb somewhat.

"Normally I would put something on this to keep you from being able to use your hand. If you were a kid, or teenager especially. But I'm going to trust you on this."

"All right. So I'll just come see you if the stitches don't hold?"

She laughed, then said, "That's probably not very funny. Doctors have lost their practices over people suing for stupid stuff. I didn't have you sign anything. Please don't sue me," she said, still laughing but sounding serious at the same time.

He didn't know how she did it, but he got her message plain and clear. She was doing her best, and for him to sue her when she was doing him a favor was absolutely ridiculous.

"I understand that some people are like that, but to do me a favor, save me a trip to the ER, or at the very least reduce the chance of infection in my hand. I appreciate it."

"No problem. Living with a doctor has benefits, so maybe you can knock a little off my rent next month."

He opened his mouth to tell her that she wasn't paying any rent, and then he realized that she was joking again.

He must be still more woozy than he thought.

"She makes a joke."

"Doctors can have a sense of humor too," she said with a sassy little toss of her head.

She started cleaning up her things, and he tested the bandage to see what he could do with his hand.

It turned out it wasn't much, without risking having the bandage pull off.

That was just as well, it would remind him to take it easy.

"If you don't mind, I'm going to go lie down," he said. Mostly because he had been up late the night before and then had gotten up early for church, and he was exhausted. He actually wouldn't have minded sitting with her for a little bit, but he knew she was looking forward to a big day tomorrow, and while she planned on changing the clinic hours to ten to seven, they still were from 8:30 to 4:30, so she wouldn't be getting up super early, but early enough. Especially if she was walking to work.

"I don't mind at all. Stitches are easy," she said.

"I really do appreciate it," he said, ignoring the fact that he didn't appreciate it to begin with. But she had been kind, hadn't grilled him too much, and had just assumed that since she could, she would.

"Let me know how much I owe you, okay?"

"I told you, you can take it off my rent."

"I'm serious. I don't want you to do this without me paying you. These things cost money." He had no idea how much novocaine cost. He'd never ordered any. Normal people couldn't get it. There definitely were perks to having a doctor in the house.

"If you let me pay rent, I'll bill you for the care."

He had no idea whether he should take her up on that or not. Maybe he should ask her how much it might cost in her practice, but he decided he'd rather go and lie down. Maybe it was the blood or just the combination of no sleep, but he found himself eager to put his feet up.

"Let me give you a hand, at least to your door," she said as he stood and gripped the table for support.

That time, she put his bandaged arm around her shoulder and put her arm around his waist. He was able to put his hand on the wall to steady himself and didn't have to lean on her too much.

"If I don't see you in the morning, I hope you have a good first day in your clinic." He really did. He wished her the very best. He wished her even more and wished for himself that she would see him as more than just a...landlord? She probably thought of him as a drifter, someone who couldn't keep a steady job, or something like that. He didn't even know. And for him, every time he saw her, he had to fight to keep his eyes off her. Or to keep them from landing on her and staying there.

They couldn't be more different.

Chapter Seventeen

Social media post on Mistletoe Meadows official site by admin:

Hello neighbors and residents of Mistletoe Meadows, I'm excited to let you know that we had another episode of the Secret Saint and his charitable projects. If you haven't noticed, maybe you didn't know that Mr. Gregory has been laid up, and it looked like the Christmas decorations were not going to be put up around town. The township had not decided what to do, but Secret Saint to the rescue. Decorations on Main Street are up and working, and this reporter thinks that it won't be long until the rest of them are up as well.

Photo of Main Street with the Christmas lights up. Photo credit: Dr. Terry McBride

❄

"*I*'ve heard Dr. Vivik's wife is doing terribly. I saw them in church on Sunday, and she looked just awful." Mrs. Hoover sat on the exam table, her hair perfectly coiffured and her glasses perched on her nose, with a silver chain that hooked on one end and went around her neck before hooking on the other.

Terry nodded. She heard this at least seventeen times today, from basically every patient she saw and sometimes from the folks who came with them as well.

It had gotten hard to think of something to say other than, "I saw them, too, and you're right. She looks frail."

She didn't want to gossip about the doctor and his wife, and she felt like she was being pumped for information. She was glad that she hadn't spoken to them any more than what she had. She would have had a hard time trying to say that she didn't know when she did, and she wouldn't want to lie. But what else was there to say?

Go visit them? Send him a note, and see if he writes back?

She didn't even know what they might need. Other than healing obviously.

"All right, Mrs. Hoover. I'm going to call in this prescription, and it should clear up that sinus infection in no time. But if it doesn't, you give my office a call, and we'll make sure that you get back in here for something different. You've had this antibiotic several times already, and it's usually effective, but there's always that chance."

"I just want to get rid of it. The holidays are right around the corner, and I do not want to be sick over Thanksgiving and Christmas."

Terry nodded, typing on her iPad and making sure that she did everything accurately. She messed a couple of things up, but her administrative assistant, Camille, and her nurse, Ashley, had both been great. Dr. Vivik had said that they were both excellent. And he had been right on the money. She'd been in contact with them several times before she had come, but not nearly as much as what she wanted to be. Still, they were helping her learn the ropes and had been patient when she'd not done everything perfectly.

She only had another hour until closing, but they would probably end up working a while after that until they got all the patients seen, since she'd been a little slow.

"Do you have any more questions for me?" she asked as she straightened up from the chair and stood, watching Mrs. Hoover.

"No, dear. Thank you very much for seeing me immediately."

"Not a problem. Call anytime," she said. She had a couple of people cancel, and one that didn't show. They were still going to bill the one that didn't show, but collecting the money could be tricky. They said right on their literature that if an appointment wasn't canceled twenty-four hours prior, they reserved the right to bill them for the missed appointment. And this appointment hadn't been canceled at all. However, Camille had told her that they typically called the day before and reminded people of their appointments. A lot of their patients were older and couldn't keep track of when they were supposed to do what.

So maybe they wouldn't bill them, but she would make sure from now on that the calls went out, and if people didn't cancel and didn't show up, they were going to get billed.

She nodded her head, just to confirm, although she doubted that she'd ever do it. She just didn't have a heart for it.

It was hard enough to bill people for their actual appointments. It felt like kicking someone when they were down to demand money from them when they were sick. That was one thing that she hadn't considered when she decided to do her own practice. Someone else had always been in charge of billing wherever she worked before. This was her first experience with it. Dr. Vivik had walked her through it and had told her he would be available to answer any questions. She wasn't afraid to ask him, although she did want to make sure that it was a legitimate question before she bothered him considering the condition of his wife.

She walked out and checked her iPad for the next patient's room and looked at their chart on her iPad before she knocked softly and walked into the room.

"Hello, Mrs. Dylan," she said as she walked in. She remembered Mrs. Dylan from the cafeteria at school.

"They told me that Dr. Vivik wasn't going to be in and I was going to be seeing a new doc, and I heard through the grapevine that was going to be you, Terry. But I just didn't believe it. Imagine, all those years ago you were in school, in the lunch line, and now here you are, my doctor."

"Well, it's a privilege to be your doctor, Mrs. Dylan. And it's good to see you today. This is just a checkup, right?"

"It is, although I expect you're going to be ordering blood work for me, since I lost my paper and didn't go in and get it done before I came."

"That's not a problem. We'll get you an order in, and you can get it done anytime it suits you in the next thirty days. Will that work?"

"It sure will, although who knows what could happen in the next thirty days. Why you heard that the Secret Saint has already done another good deed, and it's not even after Thanksgiving!"

"You're talking about the lights on Main Street," Terry said without looking up from her iPad where she typed, sending a message to her nurse asking for her to order blood work for this patient.

"No. That's old news."

"Really?" She lifted her head. She was supposed to be the reporter on the Secret Saint, and this was the first whiff she had that something new had happened. "What?"

"Well, things have been going on. The first is, Mrs. Rosario claims that the Secret Saint came and got the squirrel out of her house. I'm not sure I believe that, because I heard that her grandson was the one who got it out, and she does have a tendency to exaggerate."

"All right," Terry said, thinking about Judd after the mention of the squirrel. Interesting that she hadn't really thought about squirrels before. Now all of a sudden, every day she heard about a different one.

"And we also heard that Bethany Vance's niece had a nice little gift delivered to her house this morning. It was a medical bed. One that they hadn't been able to afford to buy, and they hadn't been able to get one through any of the other insurance providers. It was a very timely gift, and I have to say whoever the Secret Saint is, they are very well-connected."

"Wow. I'd say they're connected. I've known about Bethany's niece, but I hadn't realized that she needed a medical bed." That was a detail that whoever was the Secret Saint had been able to finagle, and she hadn't. Interesting.

She wondered again who it could be, but before she set her iPad down, she made a note to herself to make sure to make a post about both of those things. Whether the Secret Saint had gotten the squirrel out or not, she could leave it as an open-ended question. It didn't say that she had to present only cold, hard facts. It was supposed to be a fun thing that helped the community band together.

"Well, they have one now, and there was a note on it that said that it would be paid for as long as they needed it, and gave an address and a phone number for where they could call whenever they needed to send it back. It was signed the Secret Saint." Mrs. Dylan had lowered her voice and leaned forward like she was giving a particularly juicy morsel of gossip.

Terry resisted the urge to ask her to straighten up so she didn't fall off the exam table.

"Wow. I love this town," Terry said, realizing that she didn't have good news like this at any of the other places she'd worked. It really brightened people's day to hear about good things that were going on, and it made her especially happy that Mrs. Tucker had hunted her down and asked her to do it, because she actually had to focus on it.

God obviously knew that she was going to need good news in her practice. Because she'd already had to tell someone today that they had cancer and tell someone else that their scan had shown an abnormality and they needed to go back.

Another person had been sent immediately to the ER, because her symptoms mimicked a heart attack, and she had no idea what they were doing in the clinic, other than people sometimes did that. Thinking that any health place could provide the same level of care, and they didn't realize that the clinic was much, much different than an emergency room.

She wanted to shout from the housetops, "If you think you're having a heart attack, go to the ER!"

Regardless, it hadn't been an easy day. But she supposed it had been typical. And she was going to have to get used to it.

Checkups were the best though. She made good money from them, and they weren't hard.

"All right, all the stats the nurse gave me look good. Your blood pressure is within a normal range, and I don't think we're going to change your medication for that. We'll see what your cholesterol levels are when we get the blood work back. They were a little high last time."

She continued to work, finishing up with Mrs. Dylan and ending her day on a positive note, doing a physical for a kid who was going to get his driver's license. That was fun, to see the excitement in his eyes and to remember how she had felt when she was finally able to drive. It had been a good time.

She smiled again as she locked the door and walked away from her clinic. Camille and Ashley had left almost as soon as the day had been over, but she had stayed, making sure everything was prepped for the next day and thinking about the few mistakes that she'd made, things she wanted to do better. She supposed eventually it would become a routine job for her, but she didn't want to not do her very best.

As she stepped away from the clinic and contemplated the walk home, she thought about what she was going to stop and get for supper, and then she remembered. She didn't have to cook supper. Judd was going to do it. And she was looking forward to it.

Chapter Eighteen

*J*udd stood at the stove, glancing at the clock. It was almost six. And he expected Terry to be home at any time. He'd made his poppy seed chicken and was hoping that she would let him know if it was good enough for him to take to her family's Thanksgiving. Since his parents' Thanksgiving was a little bit later, he figured he could do two, although he wouldn't be expected to eat a lot at his parents' place. His mom probably wouldn't even notice if he ate anything.

He wondered what they'd do if he brought Terry.

His mom wasn't demanding that he be with anyone, but her question as to whether or not he liked men had been a little... irritating. Disappointing, maybe even hurtful.

He couldn't wait to find out how Terry's day had been, and he hoped that she wouldn't notice that he'd been bleeding under his bandage.

She hadn't left any extra bandages, maybe because she had assumed that if he needed any help, she could do it herself. Or maybe she just hadn't thought about it. Or maybe he should have bought his own. But by the time he was done working today, he hadn't had time to go to the store.

So, he just did what he could to hide it, putting a glove over top of it, which didn't really help. The bloody parts kind of stuck to the glove and were emphasized by the fact that they looked a little wet and obviously red.

Anyway, maybe she would be so excited about her first day at the clinic that she wouldn't notice.

He heard the door rattle, and his heart skipped several beats. His hands started to sweat.

He almost laughed. Why did she have that effect on him?

"Something smells amazing," she said as she came in the door.

"I almost texted you and asked if you like poppy seeds, but then I realized that I'd never gotten your contact info." He spoke while he was opening the oven, using mitts to pull out the casserole.

"I'm sorry. I can fix that right now. If you give me your number."

"I didn't mean to jump on you the second you got home. I wanted to know how your day was."

"It was fabulous." There was no doubt that there was a huge amount of happiness in her tone.

"Boy, I don't know if you're sincere," he teased.

She was grinning from ear to ear as she walked in the kitchen, pulling off her coat and shoving her gloves in her pockets. "I know that this will wear off, but I am thrilled. It feels so good to be able to go into your own clinic, talk to people as long as you want to, and just be a part of the community. I've been missing this for so long."

He didn't doubt it. She disappeared down the hall to hang up her coat and then came back to the kitchen and went directly to the sink.

"It's so much different treating people from a small town. They come in, and they're chatting about their day and what is going on, and even more so from my hometown, because most of the people that I saw today knew me."

"A good reason to have a good reputation."

"Amen!" she exclaimed.

They both laughed. "I know you do, because I knew you in high school, and I don't think there's anyone who had a better one."

"Thank you. I appreciate that." She came over and stood at his elbow, sniffing the casserole. "Man, I don't know what that is, but you can make that all day long."

"Watch it, my head's going to get too big to fit in the doorway," he said as he pulled the foil off and then grabbed the dish to take it to the table.

She moved to the cupboard and pulled out two plates. The plates clanked as she pulled out the drawer and put silverware on them, and then carried them to the table.

He had gone back and taken the oven mitts off, and tried not to be obvious about hiding his hand as he came back to the table.

She must have been looking for it, because she gasped immediately. "Your hand is bleeding!"

"I'm sorry. I was going to change the bandage, but you didn't leave any extra and I didn't have time to stop and go to the store and grab some and still have supper ready in time. So I just skipped it."

"Oh my goodness. I'm so sorry. I never thought about leaving extra bandages. But I certainly could have."

"You weren't charging before, and I would have felt bad if you left them and I hadn't paid."

"What did you do to your hand to make it bleed?" She had come over and taken a hold of his hand and held it up for her inspection.

The blood had definitely gone through the bandages.

"I bet you popped a stitch. At least one. Maybe more. What in the world have you done?"

"Well, I do work a little, sometimes," he said softly. He didn't want to be rude, but he needed to be on the job. She would too. She only wanted the best for him. "I can't just not work," he said, looking down into her eyes and hoping that at the very least she understood that he hadn't been deliberately disobeying her or not caring about the work she'd done on him. He did. Truly.

But he had to do some yard work for some elderly ladies in town, and Wilson had found out that they were going to be out of town today, and he had wanted to get it done.

Plus, tonight, if everything went well, he'd be putting the Christmas decorations up, so it was likely that he would be using his hand even more than he had today. Of course, he wasn't going to tell her that.

She nodded with her lips pressed together. "I guess there's no point stitching it up if you're just going to break them again."

"I'm not doing it on purpose. I promise. I respect your work and your orders, but at the same time, there are certain things I have to do."

She nodded, and her lips relaxed slightly, like she understood what he was saying. He wasn't trying to be disrespectful.

"All right. Are you going to be okay if I unwrap this?"

He put his good hand on top of hers as she started to unpin the bandage. Stopping her. She looked up at him, and he lifted his brows.

"Doc, you had a big day. Sit down, eat some supper. Take care of yourself. My hand will be here whenever you get done. I promise."

He wanted to take care of her. He didn't want her to work herself into the ground, and especially not for him.

She tilted her head, and then her lips moved up slightly.

"That's nice. The first time all day someone took care of me instead of the other way around. I...appreciate it." She nodded her head, and while he knew that she reluctantly listened to him, he also believed that she truly did appreciate his care and concern.

She tugged her hand out from under his, slowly, and it almost gave him the impression that she really didn't want to.

He didn't know about her, but he liked the way their hands felt together, the way his skin rubbed against hers, and the closeness of their positions.

All things he really shouldn't be thinking about. She was a doctor, for goodness' sake. And he had chosen to be what he was, but in society's eyes, it wasn't much.

Without saying anything more, she went over and sat down.

Chapter Nineteen

"Amy!" Terry said as she answered the phone, already checking to see that it was her sister who called.

"I missed your call earlier. I wanted to see how your first day went."

"I hoped that was what you're calling for."

"It was."

"I just wanted you to know that it was a great day. And I want to thank you again for all your support. It's so nice to be back in town where I have family. I missed it so much."

"I don't think you can grow up with six siblings and not feel the hole that's left when you leave them."

"I agree. It definitely leaves a void."

"I don't care if I never find that out. So, tell me about your day," she said, sounding like she had all the time in the world, which Terry appreciated. Sometimes when she talked to people on the phone, they acted like they didn't have time to talk, but Amy was never like that. Maybe that was one of the reasons why she enjoyed talking to her so much. She always had time for whatever Terry needed. Terry tried not to take advantage of that, but she appreciated it.

After she had chatted about her day for a bit, there was a lull in the conversation, and she said something that had been bothering her since church the day before.

"So... I saw you and Judd together on the wagon taking the kids."

"Wasn't that an awesome idea?" Amy said, sounding excited. "The kids are eager to come to church. It's a novel thing to get brought in a horse-drawn wagon. Super neat, and they love it."

"You do a great job of keeping them entertained. And Judd follows your lead. You guys work so well together."

"He's like a brother to me," Amy said offhandedly. "But what I was saying was, Judd had the idea, and I thought it was awesome. I couldn't wait to give him a hand with it."

"Right. I agree it was a good idea." She paused for a moment and then took a breath. "About you and Judd?"

"What?" Amy said, and she could almost imagine her walking somewhere and drawing herself up short, giving all of her attention to her phone. "What about Judd and me? Not that there is any Judd and me."

"I was just checking. You guys seem like you...enjoy each other's company."

"We do. But it almost sounds like you're insinuating that there's something more, and there's not. Judd is nice, but he's not...husband material for me. Now, his personality seems like it would match yours perfectly. Not that you're the same, but that your differences would be beneficial to both of you."

"What?" Terry said, surprised that her sister would even go there. It was one thing for her to feel a little bit of attraction, it was another thing for her sister to make suggestions like that.

"I just could see the two of you together. I saw you sitting there together at dinner yesterday, and I don't know, there just seems to be something that travels between you two. I'm not sure how to explain it. But don't worry about me. Judd is absolutely not on my radar. At all."

"All right. I guess I was just wondering." Her mind was spinning.

Amy had seen something between them? Really? So it wasn't just her imagination? Or wasn't just her feeling something intangible, but there was something that other people could see?

She could hardly believe it, but Amy hadn't been joking, although she hadn't pushed Terry in that direction either. She just made a statement that had rocked Terry's world.

"You know, you can take my place on the wagon. In fact, I think that would be fun for you and Judd to do together."

"First of all, I could never do as good a job as what you do. The kids love you, and secondly, you have Jones to give you a hand. Judd would be driving."

"True. And Jones is really good with kids. He'll make a great dad someday. I keep telling him that, and he keeps brushing me off saying something about wanting to get his practice established or something. Doesn't he know I want to be an aunt soon?"

"I don't know if he knows that or not," Terry said, thinking to herself that Amy and Jones were blind to each other and they shouldn't be.

"What are you bringing to Thanksgiving?" she asked, changing the subject.

"I'm hoping to bring my filling balls, if I can get them done. It's been really busy around here. The guys are finishing an addition, and I'm hoping to be able to take in boarders. It would be nice to have it done over the holidays, because I'm sure that's a busy time, but hopefully it'll be done soon."

Her voice wasn't quite as exuberant as it had been, and Terry wondered again if maybe the lost funding weighed heavily on her mind. She decided she would just ask.

"Is everything okay?"

"Everything's fine," Amy said with what Terry suspected was forced cheerfulness.

"How are things financially? That must be such a stress trying to figure out how you're going to feed the animals every week."

"Yeah. It's a little bit harder lately, since we lost some major funding, but God will provide. He always does."

"That's true, He does," Terry said, but sometimes it was a real test of faith to be patient and wait on the Lord. It wasn't easy, but Amy seemed to be taking it well.

"All right, I hope you have another amazing day tomorrow. If anything good happens, let me know, okay?" Amy said.

"And you let me know if you hear anything about the Secret Saint. I've been trying to keep up with all the gossip, and I'm pretty sure with my practice open, it's going to be a lot easier."

"All right, it's a deal," Amy said.

They hung up, and Terry picked up her phone and made a social media post.

Chapter Twenty

Social media post for Mistletoe Meadows:

It's me again! Happy Holidays. Thanksgiving is just two days away. Still, the Secret Saint was at it again, because overnight the rest of the Christmas decorations were put up around town. I have some pretty good contacts, but none of them can tell me that they've gotten a glimpse of the Secret Saint in his community endeavors. Does anyone else have any ideas of who it might be? Or where he might strike next?

Picture of Mistletoe Meadows holiday lights (it's pretty dark, but you get the idea). Photo credit: Dr. Terry McBride

Social media post for Mistletoe Meadows:

Happy Thanksgiving, folks! I hope you all had a great one. I learned today that five different houses in town were bombed by the Secret Saint. Gift packages were left outside doors where residents would be sure to find them. The packaging is quite unique, and each package was left with a

note signed Merry Christmas — Secret Saint. A couple of them had suggestions that they might pass it on.

Two days after Thanksgiving
Social media post for Mistletoe Meadows:

The Secret Saint has been at it again. A local restaurant was instructed to deliver meals to ten different houses on Thanksgiving. Those houses just happen to contain folks who might not otherwise have had one. The Secret Saint has struck again.

December 1
Social media post for Mistletoe Meadows:

This just in about the Secret Saint.

Word on the street is that the Secret Saint kept the parking meters full of coins on Black Friday, so anyone shopping along Main Street did not have to pay for parking. That seems like a small thing, but what a great idea, and so very kind. I'm still not getting any ideas of who this person might be. Or is there more than one?

December 4
Social media post for Mistletoe Meadows:

Another update about the Secret Saint. Not a lot of people have been hearing about this, so I had to confirm with the utility company in town. It seems that several well-deserving families have had their utility bills paid for the entirety of November and a credit put on their account for the entirety of December. This reporter was able to speak with a representative for the company, who was unable to confirm the identity of the Secret Saint. They spoke on condition of anonymity, and they refused to make speculation as to who it might be. With heating costs rising, this was a true Christmas gift for all the families involved.

Picture of electric lines outside of Mistletoe Meadows. Photo credit: Dr. Terry McBride

December 5
Social media post for Mistletoe Meadows:

And yet another Secret Saint sighting. The school bills of fifteen children at the local Christian Academy have been paid through the end of the school year. One mother said that it prevented them from having to take their children out of Christian school and put them back in public school. She does not know who the Secret Saint is, but she wished to convey her deepest gratitude. Secret Saint, if you're reading, you made a difference in people's lives. Thank you.

Picture of back of Christian school. It's a little blurry because I was late for work and took it from my car. Photo credit: Dr. Terry McBride

December 5
Social media post for Mistletoe Meadows:

We have an actual sighting!

The Secret Saint was sighted walking near Judd Landis's duplex. My informant, who spoke on condition of anonymity, claimed they had seen the Secret Saint dropping off a Christmas tree in the yard of one of the houses on that street. Its windows were still dark, and the occupants had not been able to afford a tree. Indeed, this confirms other reports I have of up to a dozen and a half other families each receiving a Christmas tree outside their house. In every instance, the family had not been able to afford to purchase the tree and were going to do without.

My anonymous source said that it looked like there might have been a small bandage on the Secret Saint's hand. But they couldn't be sure.

Nonetheless, the Secret Saint walked by Judd Landis's house and disappeared into the woods on the outskirts of town. Is it possible that the Secret Saint is also Bigfoot?

Stock photo of woods, since no photo of Bigfoot could be procured. Photo credit: Dr.

Terry McBride

Chapter Twenty-One

 *J*udd stared at his phone. He'd taken to following the posts on the Mistletoe Meadows social media site, just because he knew Terry wrote them. Sometimes they were funny, sometimes they confirmed what he already knew, and sometimes she got the details a little bit wrong. Considering that she was mostly depending on secondhand sources, that didn't surprise him a whole lot.

To his surprise, sometimes the things that he had done were exaggerated. Although, most often the numbers were too low. Which was just fine by him. But they made it more difficult for him to do the things that he wanted to do, since she had pretty much put a bull's-eye on his back. He had almost gotten busted the previous night. Or early morning, more accurately. He had seen the person in the bushes just in the nick of time. And he had to admit that the spin that Terry had put on it was hilarious.

Regardless, he had hidden in the woods and waited for more than thirty minutes before he'd come in. And he'd passed Terry on the way.

She had been heading out to work early, probably because of a call, although he hadn't been there, and she didn't say. Just nodded at him, said good morning, and walked out.

Sometime during the day, she heard the story, and as he checked the timer on the oven and glanced at his phone again, he wondered if she had put two and two together and gotten the correct answer.

He kind of felt like she probably had.

That was why he made her favorite, the poppy seed chicken that he'd made ten days ago. He'd also made it for their family's Thanksgiving. Tonight, he was hoping that it might take her mind off the idea that if she looked at the facts closely, the Secret Saint could possibly be him.

If she asked him point blank, he wasn't sure what he was going to say.

It was 6:02. She was hardly ever later than that and often a lot earlier. He knew she hoped to have their office hours changed by March of the next year, and while he had never eaten supper as late as eight o'clock, he figured that he could get used to it, because he had definitely gotten used to having Terry around.

She hadn't mentioned looking for another place to live, and he hadn't mentioned it either. He didn't want to ask, because he didn't want her to think that he was trying to push her out.

But secretly, he was hoping that she was going to stay.

He heard the familiar rattle of the door and turned the oven off, opening the door and pulling the casserole dish out of the oven.

"Hey there," he called, when she didn't say anything.

"Hey," she said, sounding subdued. Or maybe just preoccupied.

"Is everything okay?" he asked, figuring that he would try to play it cool.

"Yeah. Everything is just great. It's time for your stitches to come out." She walked into the kitchen, having already hung up her coat, and set a few things that she had in her hand down on the table.

"I forgot about them."

"I know. I wasn't expecting you to remember, but you never did stop into the clinic for your shot, so I took the liberty of bringing home a tetanus shot as well. If you have a thing about vaccinations, it's fine, just let me know. But I highly recommend one."

"I'll take any vaccination that you highly recommend, but I would prefer not to have any more than I have to have."

"That's probably a wise decision. This will keep you from dying. Tetanus can be fatal, so this is probably a good decision. Something that has less of a chance of having complications could be more of a discussion."

"Thanks for understanding," he said, not expecting her to have that view. "Didn't med school brainwash you?"

She laughed. "They probably did about a bunch of things, but I guess I just believe in free choice more than I believe in forcing things on people that they don't really want or understand. Mainly I believe in education, but I still believe in allowing people to choose for themselves. After all, God allows us to choose. He even allows us to choose whether or not we follow Him. Who am I to demand you have a vaccination?"

"I can see how it might help hospitals and other providers to be able to put resources where they're needed and not throw them at something that is an unnecessary waste."

"That's a good point. And I agree with it. Like I said, there's two sides, and I don't know that either one is absolutely correct."

"We don't have to solve that problem tonight."

"That's right. I'll give you this shot and get your stitches out, and I'll have accomplished my purpose for the evening."

"I was hoping you might want to sit by the fire some tonight," he said, turning back to face the stove, although there was nothing more for him to do there, so his hands felt a little extraneous as he struggled to find something to do with them.

He held his breath.

"I'd love that."

He smiled, sighed, and then said something he thought would be easier. "If you'd like, we can do it on your side, since my side's a little messy right now."

"Okay. Sure."

"When we're done, I'll put the fire out and leave the logs in such a way that it will be easy for you to make a fire if you so choose without me."

"I probably won't do it without you, but I was thinking about putting up a Christmas tree."

"You were?" He hadn't even thought about that. He'd bought Christmas trees at the local tree farm, just to give them business and to brighten a few families' days. He had known that there were some people who weren't buying one because they couldn't afford it, or because they couldn't put it up themselves. Wilson had been taking care of that, hiring some teenagers to volunteer to help put up the trees that had appeared and paying them for their time.

He could have gotten a tree for Terry if he had known. Goodness, he could even have put it up for her.

"I know you don't get out and around very much during the week, so if you'd like for me to grab a tree and bring it here for you so that you can put it up this weekend, I'd be happy to."

"Do you have a tree?" she asked.

"No. With it just being just me, it seems silly to put a tree up." He paused. "But I'd be happy to help you decorate yours."

He couldn't really put a tree up in his living room because he had all the things that he was using to deliver the Secret Saint gifts spread out on the floor. Wrapping paper, tape and scissors, and various gifts that he had gotten but hadn't gotten delivered yet and other things like that. He also had his notebook in there where he kept his ideas, the things he'd overheard, and a list of people that he wanted to try to figure out how he could help them.

Sometimes that was the hardest thing; knowing that someone needed help and knowing what to do to help them were often two very different things.

Regardless, if she had insisted that they go to his living room, he could have cleaned everything up, but he usually just let everything lay around because the only thing he did in there currently was work on his Secret Saint stuff. So there was no point in gathering it all up and putting it away only to get it back out again when he needed it.

"I like that," she said, and it took another moment to remember that she was talking about the Christmas tree.

"There was a big pause there. You don't have to if you don't want to." He wanted her to want to be with him. Not to be with him because she didn't have a choice.

"Oh, I want to, I just wondered why you didn't have a tree, and it sounds like you're not planning on getting one either."

"I guess I like Christmas, but I like to sit and contemplate what it means. I don't really care for all the trappings that surround it all the time."

"You're a grinch!" she said, smiling, but there was something else in her eyes. Something a little calculating, and he remembered that she had seen him in the hallway. Had known that something had been happening overnight, and the description sounded an awful lot like him.

She set the table while they had been talking, and he put the poppy seed casserole down. She got the glasses, and he put a couple of ice cubes in each one while she filled them up with water.

"Poppy seed casserole again. I guess you must know that's my favorite."

"I knew you liked it, and I don't want you to get tired of it, but I really love it as well."

There were other things he liked better, but it was fun to eat something that the person sitting across from him enjoyed, watching how much she appreciated it and thinking about how nice it felt to do something kind for her after her hard day of work.

"If you don't mind, I'll give you the tetanus shot before we eat. Not to ruin your appetite or anything, just because it's supposed to be refrigerated."

"That's fine." He didn't care when she gave it to him. As long as he didn't have to see blood. Which, he wasn't even going to say, because he figured she at least knew how to give a shot, although come to think of it, that was typically the nurse's job.

"Would you mind taking your sweatshirt off? I would prefer to give it in your upper arm if possible."

"Oh yeah. Of course."

He pulled his shirt off and held his arm out, not the one with the bandage. It was kind of hidden underneath his sweatshirt. It probably had healed slower because he had popped some of his stitches, which she had generously re-stitched.

But she was right that the stitches were ready to come out.

Turning his head to see what she was doing, he saw that she was staring at his arm.

As he turned his head, she lifted her eyes, and he couldn't read what was in them, but she seemed almost...a little dazed. A little... was that attraction?

Whatever it was, it made his mouth go dry as he stared at her, not even knowing what he was waiting for, waiting for something.

He didn't know how many seconds passed, it felt like an eternity, and he was just about ready to lift his hand and smooth it over her hair, or preferably wrap it around her shoulders and bring her closer, but she shook her head.

"I'm sorry, I got sidetracked there for a second. Here, give me your arm." Her voice sounded a little shaky, but there was also some humor in it, like she was amused at herself for being so...what? He wasn't sure. He definitely didn't want to stop staring at her though.

She had given him the shot and said, "All right. That's it," and turned, before he moved again.

He watched her put the cap back on the needle and grab a bandage.

"I'll just stick this over it, not because I expect it to bleed or anything, but just so you don't get any bacteria in there while it's clotting."

"Alright," he said, not having moved at all.

Her fingers were cool on his arm, and he found himself unable to swallow. She had her head bent and was watching what she was doing, but he noticed that she fumbled with the bandage, which seemed odd.

Were her hands trembling?

He was pretty sure if she lifted her hands up, he would find out they were.

What was going on?

If it were any other woman, he would have a pretty good idea of what was happening, but this was Dr. Terry McBride. And she couldn't possibly be the slightest bit interested in a man like him. And he could not hope to catch the attention of a woman like her, so why would he even try? Except, it seemed very interesting how God had turned the events and how right it felt between the two of them. Was that because he wanted it? Or because God did?

Chapter Twenty-Two

*J*erry sat in front of the crackling fire, some medical journals on her lap. She needed to keep up with all of the latest, and she often used her time in the evening to read and study, wanting to keep up on everything to give the best care for her patients.

But she wasn't looking at the medical journals now.

Why hadn't she confronted Judd?

She glanced across at the other chair where he sat, his feet propped up on a box, his phone in his hand where he had been reading a book, but it lay on his chest now and he breathed deeply and evenly.

He looked younger in sleep. Boyish almost. She smiled at how adorable he was, even though he would probably be embarrassed if he knew she was staring at him with his mouth open and his head tilted at an odd angle.

He was such a good man. He hadn't missed a meal since he'd said that he would cook, other than Thanksgiving, of course. He'd gone to his parents' house. She kind of wished that he'd asked her to go, but it didn't surprise her that he didn't. Why would he? It was just that he had gone to her family's Thanksgiving.

Regardless, she had come into the house tonight with every intention of asking him immediately if he was the Secret Saint. If he had been out the night before putting Christmas trees on people's porches, if that was why he smelled like pine and why the description that she had gotten from Mr. Collins had matched almost exactly Judd's description. A lot of people didn't know he had hurt his hand because he wore gloves when he was working, and it might not be common knowledge around town since the only way it would get out would be if she said it. And she certainly hadn't talked about it.

She doubted he would, and that was the thing that gave her doubt. He didn't really talk to a whole lot of people. Sure, he got around, but he had to get to know someone before he really chatted with them. She hadn't seen him standing around talking, and he never asked her for any information. If he were the Secret Saint, wouldn't he be digging for info every day on who needed money and who needed gifts and what she thought he could do that would be a blessing to people?

Wouldn't he need to get that information from a whole pile of different people, and he would be talking to everyone he met about it, right? Except, Judd had never asked her, not even one time, not even a question close to anything personal about her patients.

She wouldn't be able to tell him anyway, because the personal information of patients was private.

She could tell him any town gossip she heard, but he hadn't even asked for that.

But that wasn't really the reason she hadn't asked him.

She shifted the journals in her lap, preferring to have the paper version for as long as she could. There was just something about holding it in her hand and being able to work on it with a pencil or pen if she needed to that made her feel like she could learn the information better.

She thought that the reason that she hadn't asked him was… because she didn't really want to know.

Chapter Twenty-Three

"*A*re you coming home for Christmas? I was really hoping the whole family would be there." Terry held the phone to her ear, standing in the office of her clinic. She wasn't sure she would ever get tired of having her own office in her own clinic in her own hometown. She definitely was enjoying it today, except...there was something wrong with Isadora, her youngest sister.

"No. I just can't."

"Why?" Terry said, hearing the distress in her sister's voice but unable to think of a reason for it. It was true she was pregnant, and she did have a one-year-old and a three-year-old, so her life had to be crazy and hard and tiring and all the things that happened with raising little humans. It was so hard.

"I haven't told anyone yet, but Frederick has been cheating on me."

"No!" Terry drew the word out, pain ripping through her. Her sister, her beautiful, perfect younger sister. She didn't know her very well, because she was so much younger, but she had always been so happy and cheerful, so cute with the little pigtails and the big blue eyes and the chubby cheeks, and she'd grown into such a beautiful teenager, poised and pretty and more popular than all of her siblings. Isadora was probably the one who would call her the most often when she was in med school. Isadora had even said she wanted to be a doctor just like Terry.

And then she had met Frederick.

"Yeah. I'm devastated. Except, I think part of me suspected this for a very long time."

She wondered how long, since her sister was six or seven months pregnant.

"I just... I feel like such an idiot."

"Isadora. This is not your fault."

"I know. I understand that he didn't cheat on me because of something lacking in me, although mentally, I still feel that way. But what I'm saying is, Mom told me. She told me I was wrong."

Terry hadn't been home much, but she remembered those arguments. She got texts from both Isadora and their mom, talking about how frustrated they were with the other one. How the other one wouldn't listen, how they were insisting on their own way. Each of them said the exact same thing about the other, only Terry could see that their mom was right and Isadora was wrong.

"You even tried to tell me that Mom was right," Isadora said, as though she too were going through all the things that had been said and done at that period of time.

Terry didn't want to say it. Because Isadora was right. Their mom had told them, and Terry had said that she was right, and Isadora was so determined to be with Frederick that she wouldn't listen.

"Mom said he wasn't a Christian. She said the first rule of a relationship was to make sure that he was a Christian. She drummed that into our heads from the time I was a baby."

"Me too. Me too."

"She quoted that verse, 'be ye not unequally yoked together with unbelievers,' a million times to me. I knew it. But Frederick was older and dashing, and when he started to pay a little bit of attention to me, I was so flattered."

"I saw that you were. It started with those texts, and I know Mom knew that you were texting him and she told you to stop. She said it wasn't wise. She said you're going to end up—"

"I know. I know. I can hear it like it was yesterday. I can hear her saying that I was going to end up hurt. That sin was always found out, and that if God said that we shouldn't be unequally yoked with unbelievers, I shouldn't even open the door to the possibility that something might develop."

"Mom never would let us text people of the opposite gender. I know it's a common thing, and I thought she was so stupid and old-fashioned and untrusting, but I'm glad she didn't. Because she's right. It starts out with an innocent text, and you put one foot on the slippery slope, and then pretty soon something happens and they are the one person that responds to you, and..."

"Before long, you're telling them things that you shouldn't be, and they're responding with real sympathy, instead of telling me that I need to grow up and stop complaining and do the right thing and all the things that parents say and siblings say and people who know me say. He acted like he really cared."

"I understand that. I could see that. And I wished I could help you, but feelings are so strong. You have to have the character to see where it's going, to listen when people tell you that it's a bad idea, and to realize that they have a view that you don't have."

"I have that view now," Isadora said bitterly.

Terry was silent. She didn't want to rub anything in to her sister. She felt bad enough for her. Of course she would go back and do things differently if she could. Of course she would listen now that she knew where it was headed; she wouldn't be texting someone that she shouldn't be. Of course she would do what her mom said. But when she was younger, she just couldn't see the wisdom.

"Mom even said I would end up with small children, crying and hurt in the divorce. She said sin always hurts. She would point to her own heart and say her heart was hurting, that the sin had already started hurting her, and I just laughed. I was so stupid. How could I have been so callous?"

"You know if you go to Mom, she's not going to laugh at you."

"I deserve it. I laughed at her and thought she didn't know what I knew. I knew he was an upstanding, upright, wonderful man. So what if he wasn't a Christian? He was better than a lot of the Christians I knew!"

"Hasn't he told you that he didn't want you going to church?"

"Yes. He won't go with me. He doesn't want me to go, and he definitely didn't want me to go and dedicate our children. I wanted to, but I struggle to even be able to go on Sunday mornings, let alone any extra services."

"Those extra services are where you really learn," Terry said, knowing she'd missed more than a few of them herself because of the schedule that she had to keep in med school and residency. Also, in the city it was often hard to find a good church, especially in the Northeast where she had spent those four years.

"Oh, Terry, I can't explain to you how bad this hurts," Isadora said, sounding like she was doubled over in pain.

Terry could only hold the phone and wish that her sister was closer so she could give her a hug. "I wish I could hug you. I wish you were closer. I wish you could come home," she said.

"I can't even come home! Gilbert's there. And he has a wife who loves him, and she's dying. I can't just drop in, but I don't know what I'm going to do!"

"Do you think Frederick would be willing to apologize? Would you take him back?"

"When I confronted him about it, he told me that he wasn't attracted to me and didn't love me anymore. That I was repulsive to him and I could never be as good as this woman that he's found. She's everything that I'm not."

"Wow," Terry said, wanting to grab a hold of Frederick and rip his throat out. Hold the bloody pieces of his windpipe in her hand and squeeze it until he was dead.

That was a little violent. She tried to get a hold of herself. Just because the man had hurt her sister didn't mean that he wasn't still a child of God. It didn't mean that she shouldn't still be loving him, caring for him, praying that he would get right and get saved.

But by far, her sister was the most important thing in this equation, her sister and her children.

"I know Mom wouldn't care if you moved in, and I would feel better if you were closer." It sounded like there was no hope of reconciliation.

"I don't even know if I can do that. I just feel so...exploded. I don't know how to explain it. Just can't do anything, I can't think of anything, I can't respond, my whole world has crashed down, and it's all I can do to take care of the kids."

Terry swallowed. There were a lot of times in her life where she wished she had chosen a different career. Where she had gone in a direction where she would have more time for family and friends.

If Isadora were here, she could at least help her in the evenings and Saturday and Sunday when she wasn't at the clinic. But as it was... "I can drive out this weekend, Friday evening, and stay there until Sunday evening. I can take care of the kids."

Her sister lived near Virginia Beach, which was four hours away from Mistletoe Meadows. She could leave even Thursday night after work, if she rescheduled her Friday appointments.

"No. Don't tell anyone. I... I need to get it reconciled to myself first. I can't handle other people talking to me about it until I can deal with it myself."

"All right. Are you sure? Because I'd be happy to do that."

"I'll call Mom. Just...give me time."

She knew from personal experience, especially for emotional wounds, time was often the best healer. As long as a person could get it out of their head. The problem was, a person had to stop thinking about it. Had to stop rolling it around in their head, they had to stop and take every thought captive, which was not an easy thing to do. Especially with something like this. Thoughts of revenge, thoughts of regret, thoughts of hurt and anger and a desire to lash out and induce the pain that they had been dealt on someone else, were hard to get past. She certainly didn't expect her to get past it at this point. It was akin to someone being in a car accident and a doctor saying get up and walk, when both legs were broken. It just took time for the legs to heal.

It was going to take time for Isadora's emotions to heal.

And like broken legs, Isadora would probably never be the same again.

And the really, really hard thing was that she had been counseled not to. But she had thought that she knew better than her parents and that it was just a little thing, just a tiny bit of disobedience by marrying a man who wasn't a Christian. But now it had exploded on her, definitely on her children, and she'd already hurt her mother, and now everyone who was involved in the mess, everyone would see her pain and hurt because of her.

Terry had seen this more than once, in the volunteer work that she had done at women's shelters. There was not a high percentage of Christians in the shelters, but there were some, and to a woman they almost all said that their parents had counseled them to not begin the sin, but they thought it was harmless.

"I love you, Isadora. I'll do anything you need me to do," Terry promised, knowing that she didn't want to close her clinic, but if it meant saving her sister, she would move out there in a heartbeat.

"Thanks. I," she seemed like she was struggling, "I... I just need time."

They hung up, and Terry said a prayer for her sister, knowing that she would be praying hourly, even minute by minute for her sister to be able to heal quickly and at least take care of her children, both the two that were born and the baby she was still carrying. And Terry would do whatever she could to help.

Chapter Twenty-Four

"Oh, Terry! Terry!"

Terry had come to dread that voice. She put a smile on her face as she walked out of the church and turned to see Mrs. Tucker. "Yes?"

"Terry, you are doing a fantastic job with the social media posts on our town account. I could not be happier," she said, putting a hand on Terry's arm and making her feel like she was a teenager again, instead of in her early thirties.

"Thank you, Mrs. Tucker. It's been fun." Except the pictures. She was terrible at taking pictures.

"Those ones that you use pictures on get a lot of likes and comments." Mrs. Tucker wrinkled up her nose and muttered under her breath, "No matter how terrible the pictures are, it seems." She gave her head a little shake, and her eyes brightened again. "We've gotten a lot of new followers, and we have tourists who are interested in our town because of you." Mrs. Tucker's voice was a little singsongy, which Terry took to mean that she was happy, very happy, with her.

"And because you've done such a good job with that, I have

another big favor to ask of you," she said in such a way that Terry was pretty sure she was supposed to be honored, but she held her breath. The more honored she was supposed to be probably meant the more terrible the job was. But she would withhold judgment.

"I want to know if you and Judd Landis will man the hot chocolate competition booth after you drive the wagon in the town Christmas parade on Thursday."

"Wow. That's kind of short notice, isn't it?"

"You're right. Usually I have this planned way back in September, but my husband and I took an anniversary trip to Hawaii, and then we ended up going to Iceland to visit family I never knew I had. It has been a crazy fall, but I'm back, and I'm trying to get things organized for Christmas, because that is our jam around here."

"We celebrate Christmas year-round, because of the town name and everything," Terry said, which was true. A lot of stores kept their decorations up year-round or changed them out every month to a different Christmas scene. She lost track of the number of businesses that had twelve different decorations sets, one for each month.

"You're right. Good point. But we're going to jump into this Christmas, and that will be a great springboard for the next year. I did leave my things in the hands of people that I thought were very capable, but you know the old saying, 'if you want something done right, do it yourself.'" She smiled, like life was a trial, but she was going to power through.

Terry kind of felt like it was probably her turn to pat Mrs. Tucker's arm, but she just couldn't bring herself to do it. She would feel like an eighth grader patting the principal's arm after a scolding.

"All right, I'm going to put you down on my list," she said, getting her clipboard up and writing her name down. "Do you think you can talk to Judd for me?" she asked, like getting Judd in was as big of a deal. "I just figured since the two of you are sharing a duplex, it would be easy for you to plan. I know you're busy as a doctor and all, but he should have plenty of time. As I understand, he doesn't do that much. But at least he's not a drain on society, so I'm not going to complain, although he could go out and get a real job, which wouldn't be a bad idea for him. But who am I to say?" Mrs. Tucker said, obviously feeling like she was the person to say, and to her surprise, Terry found herself getting offended.

"Judd does a lot of things that he doesn't get credit for. He helps a lot of people. And he notices things. Like my nephew, he let him help blow the leaves in the yard."

"Any man would do that," Mrs. Tucker said, in a tone that made Terry feel like she was about two years old. "That's normal. I'm talking about actual work. Jobs. He needs a job, but we don't have to stand here in the churchyard and argue about it. But God does say that a man should provide. And I would not consider him husband material for anyone, because he obviously is incapable of providing for anyone aside from himself. And I wouldn't trust him if he said he was going to get a job because in the time that I've known him here in Mistletoe Meadows, he's never lifted a finger."

"You only moved in fifteen years ago, didn't you?"

"Yes, but that's plenty of time to observe a person and know about him."

It almost felt like Mrs. Tucker hadn't felt like Judd was worth getting to know. But she heard from other people that his parents never hung out in town. And they really didn't know anything about them. And Judd of course never said.

Terry bit her tongue to keep from arguing and insulting Mrs. Tucker. "All right, so I'm supposed to man the hot chocolate competition booth with Judd, after we take the horse-drawn wagon in the parade. Is that right?"

"That's correct. And don't forget, people love it when you throw candy. Although, as a doctor, I guess you could throw apples, except everyone knows they keep doctors away. I don't know, something healthy. Broccoli. Throw broccoli."

Mrs. Tucker waved and hurried away, and left Terry staring at her back. Broccoli?

Yes, it probably was good for a person, but even she knew that no one was going to want to pick broccoli up off the street and eat it. Not even her.

And she was supposed to ask Judd. Well, she would wait until after their Sunday lunch. Judd was with the wagon and horses currently, and he would have to come back and take care of those before he could make it out to the McBride home.

She finished walking down the steps, stopping to chat with a few friends and neighbors, before she went and grabbed the casserole she was taking to her mother's house. She was hoping that Isadora had been able to make it there. Her mom had been talking to her, saying that she didn't mind if Isadora moved back, and Gilbert had even talked to her, from what Terry understood. Telling her that his kids would love to have their cousins to play with for a bit.

The last time Terry had talked to Isadora, she hadn't wanted to admit that she was a failure—her words—and come crawling back with her tail between her legs, living with her mom.

She had been so adamant that she was doing the right thing by going with her husband, and she figured that her mom wouldn't be happy to have her divorced and living in her home after so blatantly flaunting what her mom had begged her not to do.

But Terry had assured her that their mom loved her and was only warning her, and the fact that Isadora didn't heed the warning was painful for their mom, but she of course still loved her and would happily take her in. Terry knew that to be a fact. Maybe it was because she had been away for so long, but she saw her mom through new eyes. Maybe through adult eyes, she wasn't sure.

Chapter Twenty-Five

"Oh my goodness, I can't believe this. There's more?"

Charity Amime stood in front of her house, her hand at her throat, her hair a mess, her face looking haggard and wan, but her eyes shone.

Judd nodded. "I have several more loads. I want to get them in before the kids see them, unless you're putting the gifts out before Christmas?"

"No. No, I'm not, but wow. When you said you wanted to bring some gifts over, I thought you meant like one for each child. Not five. With five kids, that's...a lot!"

Judd nodded. "Now remember, you're not allowed to tell anyone who brought them. I'm not going to come back in here and take them away, but you're going to put me out of a job. Because the person who has me doing this doesn't want anyone to know who I am, so there's less chance that they can trace him through me." That was the line he used with everyone that he absolutely had to talk to. And he hadn't had a choice with Charity.

He had twenty-five gifts for her children, and she didn't know it, but there were five gifts in there for her.

He hadn't been able to just drop them off, because her children were young and home all the time. It was likely that they would see the gifts before their mom could do anything about it.

"I won't tell a soul," Charity promised, and he was pretty sure she meant it. "How? Who? What?" she asked, like she couldn't figure out what question she wanted to start with. "Who told you about me?"

"The dude who is behind this has some pretty good contacts." That was typically what Judd said. "The dude who is behind this." It was him, but he wasn't lying whenever he spoke for himself.

Wilson helped as well, but Judd contributed all the money. Wilson was better at getting contacts, although Judd had a thing going with the pastor's wife, Bekah, and the owner of the coffee shop in town, Vivi. They were both in a position to give him all the information that he needed, and if they weren't able to get it by regular means, they could figure out how, like figuring out what gifts each one of Charity's children wanted, plus figuring out gifts that would be good for her.

"This town is awesome. You guys have been so good to me since my husband...disappeared. Didn't come back. Whatever," she said, waving her hand, like she was over it, although he doubted she was. It had only been a half a year ago that he had gone on a business trip to Japan and never come home. It had taken Charity months to track him down, through his employer, and find out that he was living with someone in Australia.

He thought he would circumvent the American system of child support, which would be huge with five children, by moving to a different country. He'd been planning it for a while. Clear back before she had her last child.

That was common knowledge throughout the town, although people didn't throw it up to Charity. She was a sweet girl who hadn't deserved what her husband had done, but Judd wasn't sure what she was going to do. Childcare was more expensive than any job that she could make any money at, and she'd been trying to work from home, to no avail.

"I want to offer to pay you, but I know I can't afford it. I have twenty bucks in my account right now."

"Well, hang on, because I have all the fixings for Christmas dinner. The turkey's frozen, but everything else should keep until then."

He turned away and walked back to the car to get another load, unable to handle watching her eyes fill with tears. His heart just broke for her, but he didn't know what else to do.

He grabbed the last of the gifts. He'd actually gotten pretty good at gift wrapping, and he carried them up the steps and into the house. She had been taking them upstairs and, he assumed, hiding them.

She hadn't said anything, and neither had he, but he also had enough cash for the next three months of rent. She might be thinking to herself right now that it was fine for her to be hiding the gifts, but if she didn't come up with the money, she was going to be out of the house before Christmas, and then it wouldn't matter where the gifts were.

The cash that he had would cover the back months of rent as well.

He went back to the car and got the grocery bags full of food. There was a brownie mix and a cake mix in there as well as eggs, which wasn't as good as a pumpkin pie, but a pumpkin pie wouldn't last until Christmas, unless it was frozen, in which case the frozen ones were usually too small for a family of that size.

It was funny the things a single man might learn when he went around town acting as a Secret Saint.

There was a little note in the bag as well, explaining everything, and that's where the cash was.

"All right, here are the grocery bags. I do want to mention that there is a note in this one, because there's something with the note and I want to make sure you get it." He didn't want people accidentally throwing money away. So, if he met people, he always told them that. Of course, most of the time he was trying as hard as he could not to meet anyone. In fact, he had waited until dusk had fallen so that he could carry these things in without anyone noticing, and if someone did, hopefully they wouldn't recognize him with his big, bulky jacket and beanie.

"Can I tell that Dr. Terry so she can put it on the town's social media? I know that no one's going to appreciate this more than me, but it might make some people feel good."

"You can tell whoever you want to about what happened, just don't mention my name, okay?" He lifted his brows and got a promise out of her. It was important to him that they promised. If they broke their promise, that was on them, but he would do what he could to be able to continue. He could do it even though people knew his name, but it made it more fun, and it made it easier for him, if he could do it and no one knew. Plus, there were bound to be people who didn't think he was fair and who would complain that someone didn't get something that they deserved, like deserving could be a thing as well.

Regardless, it was important to him to keep his identity secret from as many people as possible. There were just three who knew.

"Thank you so much. I can't do it now, but maybe someday I'll be able to pass it on."

He nodded and smiled. "I'm sure you will. Merry Christmas," he said and nodded his head again before he turned around and walked swiftly off the porch. When he waited until after dusk to do deliveries, he always worried that he wouldn't have supper ready on time. He wanted to keep his word to Terry. That was important to him. Not just keeping his word, but also because it was Terry.

He hurried home and was able to prepare the hamburger casserole that he had planned earlier in the week when he bought groceries. He'd settled into the routine of buying things on Monday to make the four meals that he was responsible for, and Terry had started going to the grocery store Friday evening and getting things to provide for the weekend. She was the one who made a meal for them to take to her mom's house, although several different times, she'd asked him to help her with the meal that she made.

He was always more than happy to oblige, not just because it was flattering to have someone ask for his recipe, which meant that she liked his food well enough to want to share it, but also because it was time spent with Terry.

He'd hit the porch just as the first snowflakes started to fall. There had been a storm in the forecast, and it was starting slightly earlier than they had expected. He hoped that Terry made it home okay from the clinic, although since she was walking, he wasn't nearly as concerned about her. Still, people died every winter because someone skidded off the road and ended up on the sidewalk striking someone with their vehicle.

He wasn't usually a worrywart, at least he didn't used to be, but he found himself listening hard until he finally heard the door rattling that signaled Terry's return.

On a whim, he had gotten the ingredients out for hot chocolate. He didn't know about her, but he hoped she would enjoy it while the snow fell, and they had planned to decorate the tree this evening as well. Although, the last few nights that they had planned to do it, something had come up either for her, a patient sick, a call to her sister, or for him, Wilson needing him for something or Amy needing them to finish more fencing so that she could book someone who had called and asked out of the blue.

He absolutely wanted to do anything that would help Amy get money, since she was struggling as well.

"Hello," Terry called as the door closed behind her.

There was a little bit of time while she took her coat off, and he could hear her shaking it over the rug to get the snow off before she hung it up.

When she finally walked in the kitchen, he was just taking his hamburger casserole out of the oven and turning off the broccoli that he had steamed on the stove.

"Is it still snowing?" he asked, looking at her white hair and assuming that it was, although it could have turned to rain. The forecast had been up and down over that.

"It is, and it's such a beautiful night," she said, smiling. "I don't know who the Secret Saint is, but I am so glad they were able to get the lights up on the side streets, because it made my walk home absolutely stunning."

When he'd been younger, on the farm, he'd always thought the prettiest times were times where the snow was falling in the woods and when it would stick to trees and over the fields. He supposed it was pretty where it fell, anywhere, even in town.

"Well, that's good. I don't know if you want some, but I made enough hot chocolate for two, and I assumed we're still on for the Christmas tree?"

"I hope so. As long as I don't have to talk to my sister again. I'm sorry about that."

"Not a problem. I'm glad you were able to stop and talk to her. I hope she's okay." She had talked a little the next night about what her sister wanted, so he knew basically that her husband had left her, cheated on her, and treated her pretty badly. He felt bad for her and knew that Terry was happy that she was coming home so she would be able to visit her and spend more time with her especially since her sister had decided to move in with her mom, possibly coming before Christmas.

"As good as can be expected, I guess. I feel so bad for her. If it were me, I think I would have trouble getting out of bed. She has two small children to take care of."

He nodded as she got the plates out the way she usually did, and he set the food on the table. Then she got water in the cups while he put ice in them, and they sat down together.

"This smells amazing. You don't know how much I appreciate opening the door and smelling supper as I step in."

"I'm glad you like it," he said, feeling somehow warm and happy inside.

He said grace as he usually did, and they started eating.

"I had a patient, Francis Kleinschmidt, who told me about a house that is for rent. I honestly stared at her for about five full seconds before I realized that she was telling me that because I'm supposed to be house hunting. I completely forgot." She rolled her eyes a little. "You probably are wondering when in the world I'm going to move out and let you have your house back, and here I haven't even been looking. You need to remind me."

He had frozen as soon as she had started talking about looking for another house.

He liked having her here. He didn't want her to leave. He... enjoyed eating with her, talking with her in the evening, spending time with her, and while he hadn't touched her since she took his bandage off and his stitches out, he'd been thinking about it. A lot.

But if she wanted to go, he didn't want to be the one standing in her way.

A few more minutes went by before she looked up and said, "You're quiet tonight." She narrowed her eyes.

"Just thinking," he said, which was true. How was he supposed to tell her that he was thinking about how he didn't want her to go? Especially if she wanted to leave.

"So do you want to talk about it?" she asked,

Judd's mouth shut, knowing that he wasn't going to be able to do anything but blurt out the truth. He couldn't approach it sensibly. "How did your day go?"

"It was great. My last patient of the day told me that Charity Amime, you know, the lady at the edge of town who has five children and her husband disappeared over the summer?"

Judd tried to look innocent and interested and surprised all at once as he nodded. It wasn't easy.

"Well, apparently the Secret Saint has visited her house and dropped off gifts for everyone in the family, including her. Plus a turkey dinner for Christmas, and gave her enough cash to pay her back rent and three more months' rent."

"Wow. That's generous."

"That's exactly what I thought," she said, looking at him with her finger on her chin.

"I guess I'd be careful giving someone like that cash. Although, Charity's a good girl. She's not going to spend it on drugs or booze."

"No. She's not, is she?" she said, looking back at her plate and spearing a piece of broccoli with her fork. "So how was your day?" she asked with a smile that he couldn't quite read.

"It was good. Cold. I rushed to get done before the snow. And I did."

"What were you doing?"

"I painted the new addition to the country market. They're hoping to get everything open by March. They have some more jobs for me later this winter."

"Interesting," she said, putting the broccoli in her mouth.

He looked back down at his plate and tried to figure out whether he would rather talk about him not wanting Terry to leave or him being the Secret Saint.

He looked up and said, "I don't want you to go."

Chapter Twenty-Six

Terry stared at Judd. She had been ready to jump him over the Secret Saint things. Her source had told her what the person who was carrying the groceries and presents into Charity's house looked like. It was getting dark, but the description sounded an awful lot like Judd. Down to his moleskin jacket.

But all of that fled out of her brain at his words.

"Out of here?" she asked, even though she knew what he was talking about. Maybe she just needed to confirm.

"Yeah. Here." He sounded almost sad, like the idea of her leaving had made him depressed.

"Well, I've taken over your kitchen, and I spend a lot of time in the bathroom, especially on the weekends, and more than once, you've had to delay your shower until the next day because I was in there, and you didn't want to ask me to get out."

"It's not a big deal. Nobody cares if I shower or not."

"I'll tell you what, I would care right now if you hadn't showered," she said seriously. She appreciated the fact that he was fastidiously clean. There were things that people could say about Judd, but that he was a slob was not one of them.

She even liked his beard. He kept it neatly trimmed, and it gave him a dashing look that she admired, and she found her eyes roaming to it anytime they were home together.

"I'll make sure I shower before supper then. As long as you're working, I shouldn't have any trouble getting in the bathroom."

"But you don't get home in time. You're trying to get as much done in the evening as I am. And there were a couple of times where I haven't been very considerate."

Once she'd gotten on the phone with Amy, talking about Isadora and what they could possibly do, when she was supposed to be doing something with Judd. And once she had taken a bath instead of a shower and had lost track of time as she soaked in the tub, and she had to admit, the main thing she'd been thinking about had been Judd.

Actually she didn't have to admit that, and she wouldn't admit it to anyone. Especially not to the man sitting across the table from her.

"I told you I don't care. It doesn't make a bit of a difference to me how much time you spend in the bathroom. I figure you've earned it. I'm hearing that people are loving the new doctor."

"Are you hearing that?" she asked, surprised. So surprised that she forgot what they were actually talking about. She'd realized that sometimes he changed the subject on purpose. He didn't seem like the kind of person who would do that, but he was, and he could be pretty slick about it too.

"I have. In fact, I haven't heard anything but good things. Sometimes it's a little bit hard for someone new to come in and fit in in a small town, but you're native, and everyone loves you. They loved you before, and I think they love you even more now."

"I wouldn't go that far. And I don't know, maybe they won't like me so much when some people get behind on their bills." She hadn't been there long enough for that to happen, but she knew that was one of the drawbacks of a small practice. Every dollar mattered, and sometimes people just couldn't, or wouldn't, pay.

He took a bite of his casserole and studied the rest of what was left on his plate like he was going to have to answer a test about it later.

"So, what were you saying? Something about you don't want me to move out?"

"Yeah." His voice was soft, and he didn't elaborate.

"So you don't need me to look for another house?"

"No. You're fine right here. I enjoy your company. I look forward to evenings with you. I would feel lonely if you left and I had to start eating by myself again. You brighten the house up somehow, even though we don't even spend every evening together." They spent most evenings together. There were a few where they'd gotten called away to other things, but if they were both home, they typically were hanging out in her living room. A couple of times, she had suggested that they go to his, but he would remind her about it being messy, and she knew at times that her mom had been embarrassed when company had stopped by and her house hadn't been perfect.

Terry had left her perfectionist side behind a long time ago, back in med school somewhere, since she knew that as a busy doctor, she just might not have a perfect house. And that was okay.

Regardless, she didn't want to make Judd uncomfortable if that's what it was.

She also noticed that he didn't say anything about having feelings for her. He just spoke about the company and companionship.

"So you were fine for the first thirty years of your life living by yourself, but now you'd be lonely?" she pressed, wanting to hear just one thing that told her that maybe he would like her for more than just friends.

"If you're asking if anyone would do, it's only you," he finally said, and his words didn't exactly answer her question, but it answered the question she thought, not the one she spoke.

She smiled a little, appeased. Although she wanted more. She'd been wanting more for a while, but she just didn't know if it was a good idea. Mrs. Tucker's words rang in her head, and she knew the entire town would be shocked if Judd and she got together.

They just didn't seem like the kind of people who would. But that didn't mean it wouldn't work.

Wait. What was she thinking? Was she seriously thinking that she might want to be more with Judd?

He had said he didn't want her to leave, but it sounded like it was more like companionship.

He made a show of looking at his phone. "Wow. If we're going to decorate the tree tonight, we probably ought to get started. I can turn the chocolate on while we're clearing off the table."

"And I can get some Christmas music up on my phone. I have a bigger speaker upstairs. I'll go get it," she said, gathering their plates and cups from the table and setting them on the sink.

He usually did the dishes on weeknights, and she typically did them when she cooked. It seemed like it would work better the other way, but that really wasn't how they did it. Honestly, most of the time they helped each other.

They just seemed to get along.

They'd never really technically divided the work, other than the cooking, everything else just happened. He usually swept and scrubbed the kitchen and bathroom and hall once when he was on cooking duty. On Tuesdays, usually. Which seemed to be a slow day for him. And then she did it all once over the weekend.

Neither one of them had said that they had to, they just did.

Too bad she couldn't have had a roommate in college like that, but she never had.

By the time she had gotten her speaker and come down and had Christmas music playing softly out of it, he stepped into the room with a hot chocolate in each hand.

"Are we gonna talk about this? Are we just gonna throw some decorations on it? Yours and mine?"

"You have decorations?" she asked, surprised. He had said that he didn't have a tree because it was just him and that type of thing, which she thought was kind of sad. But she understood when he said that he liked to think about the reason for the season. She just... enjoyed the pretty lights. She liked to look at them, contemplate them, and let the beauty sink into her soul. She thought about the reason for the season, but the lights helped get her in that celebrating, reflective mood that she only had during the Christmas season.

"I have a few. But they might not match yours. I've heard that women are kind of picky about that kind of thing."

"Oh, you have?" she asked, wondering for the first time if he had prior relationships. It was funny that she'd never considered it. She supposed she just thought that he'd been alone all his life, and since he was so quiet, it made sense that maybe he didn't have relationships.

"Occasionally I've been reminded of that."

"So is that from a prior relationship?" she asked, making sure her words sounded light and not accusatory.

"No, not really." He hesitated, blowing on his hot chocolate but not taking a sip. It was steaming, and she knew it would burn her mouth if she tried, so he probably figured the same thing. She assumed it was a stalling tactic.

Finally he said, "My mom. She was pretty picky."

"Was?" she asked, knowing that he'd said he was going to his parents' house for Thanksgiving.

"Sorry. Is. I guess I just think of it in the past, because I don't have to do Christmas with her anymore. I mean, I usually try to spend at least half a day with my parents, but she was not necessarily a fun person to be around. Because everything had to be just so. And it kind of took the fun out of everything, at least in my childish eyes."

"I can see why that would be. I don't think anyone enjoys decorating whenever you're working for someone who's impossible to please."

He nodded, so she knew her guess had been right. Interesting that he would mention that about his mom. And it made her curious.

"So, I assume they live around here?" It was funny that she had never even thought to ask about his parents before.

"Yeah. Down the mountain toward Whisker Hollow."

"Oh." She knew there were a bunch of high-dollar farms in the area, and she imagined whatever home they had was probably worth a good bit because of that. But she had assumed that he had come from a more modest, maybe even poor, area.

But maybe there were some groups of houses that she hadn't noticed. She'd have to check on her way down the next time.

"You want us to both go get our decorations and we can take a look and see what might look good together?" he asked, like he was trying to change the subject.

She'd almost forgotten that they were even going to decorate a tree. She was trying to form her next question while still trying to figure out where he lived and what exactly kind of family he'd come from.

But he was right. They could talk while they were decorating.

It didn't take long for them to both grab their decorations. His were up in the attic, but hers were under the bed where she'd stowed them when she'd moved in. She didn't have many. But she always decorated a little bit for Christmas, even if it was just some tinsel and bulbs on a windowsill. Maybe a candle.

He had a much bigger box, which was probably a good thing, since she hadn't thought to buy anything.

"You don't have much," he said, looking at her paltry supply of Christmas decorations.

"I guess I need to start collecting things. Or I can be minimalist like you are."

"I have a bigger box than you do, so you can't really complain about me."

"I wasn't complaining, and I actually think that's probably a good idea. I think we do get too wrapped up in making everything perfect, having all of our dreams come true, or whatever it is. And we definitely lose sight of the reason we celebrate."

"I wonder if that's the devil. He always seems to want to distract us from what's really important. He does that with politics too. We get so enraptured about what's going on, and so intent on telling the other side how they're wrong, that we forget that, as Christians, we're supposed to be about loving others and showing them Jesus. Not winning a political argument."

"Ouch."

They laughed a little together, but she was definitely thinking that he was absolutely correct. She got sidetracked way too easily, thinking things were important that really weren't.

They surveyed their boxes, figuring out what they thought would look best, and ended up using most of it.

"It will be a hodgepodge, but those kinds of trees can look pretty too. Maybe by next year, I'll have collected enough decorations and figured out a theme. And if you want, we can put a tree up in your living room as well, and then there will be a tree in both front windows."

She stopped. She was talking like she was going to be here next year.

She had her mouth open, but no words came out as her eyes slowly moved until they met his.

He'd noticed too.

What they had said in the kitchen earlier came back to her. He wanted her to stay. And it wasn't just anyone, it was her.

But she hadn't given any kind of response back. He had let her know that she was special to him. Special in a unique way. She wasn't just a friend, she was the friend he wanted.

She hadn't returned that, not even a little. And she didn't know what to say. Did she want to?

Immediately, her heart said yes. She wanted him to know that she had never done this type of thing with anyone before. And she was treading on entirely new ground. But it felt a little dangerous too, because she wasn't sure that she wanted to...what? Be with him?

Why not?

"So what was your dad like?" he asked, his voice a little rough. He tore his eyes away and looked at the decorations they had out in front of them, grabbing a string of lights.

"He was awesome. Fun, funny, always trying to make us all laugh. He was the perfect dad to have six kids. But he worked hard, and we didn't always have a whole lot since Mom stayed at home and raised us. I always admire that, but I guess I never really thought about doing that myself. Now I wonder why. Because the idea of having a child, I guess I'd kind of like to raise it myself too. What's the point otherwise?"

"If you give it to someone else to raise?" he said easily as he found the end of the light string and plugged it in. The lights came on. For some reason, she'd been thinking that they might not work.

"Yeah. I mean, it's your child, God's given you the responsibility to raise it, and if I'm off working, and I send it to someone else to take care of for most of its waking hours, I mean, it just seems...dumb."

"I think a lot of things we do in our society today are dumb. But we've accepted them as good or smart or necessary."

"Yeah," she said, thinking about what Mrs. Tucker had said to her in the church lot about Judd. How he should have a job and he should be making more money and he was never going to be able to take care of a family. Maybe he was just doing things differently than everyone else did. And was there any problem in that?

He was dependable, had not missed cooking a meal since he said he would, he was considerate, clean, and kind.

Did it matter that he didn't have a lot of money?

"You were talking about your dad, and somehow we got off the subject," he prompted as he started to string the lights around the tree, and she pulled a second string out.

"Well, he and Mom seemed to have a really great relationship, and I always wanted that, and I never really thought about how it probably wasn't compatible with being a doctor. Or maybe wasn't compatible with studying to be a doctor anyway. I could make being a doctor a nine-to-five job, although Dad was a truck driver, so he didn't really have a nine-to-five."

"I bet that left your mom home by herself a lot," he said, seeming to understand immediately that driving a truck wasn't a comfortable, easy job.

"Yeah. He was regional, so he wasn't gone for weeks at a time, but there were lots of overnights. Mom has stories about when us kids were little and she was home by herself, but as we got older, it was probably good for us, because she gave us a lot of responsibility at a young age, and I know that some people will say 'oh, kids shouldn't have too much responsibility, they should be able to be kids,' but I think we let our kids be kids for way too long."

"I can't disagree."

"What about you?" she asked, trying not to show how interested she actually was.

"I was an only child. I was just going to ask what it was like to grow up with a whole pile of siblings."

"It was awesome. We always had a playmate, because even if one of them was mad at you, someone else would play. Except those very rare times when everyone ganged up on one person and we were all mad at them. But usually it was because they deserved it."

"Deserved?"

"Like, I don't know, they did something that got us all in trouble. Like didn't weed the garden when they were supposed to and we all had to go out and weed their share, since Mom didn't understand that it was just them. You know? Did your mom always listen to you whenever you tried to explain stuff to her?"

"I don't remember, but I would think with your mom, six kids would take up an awful lot of time. It would probably be hard to listen to everyone explain everything. You'd never get anything else done."

"That's true. Kids often have a lot of explanations for stuff. And by explanations, I mean excuses."

He laughed, as she figured he would.

"So you're an only child? Wow. I want to ask if that was lonely, but if it was your normal, then maybe it wasn't."

"I suppose I got lonely, but I always was pretty happy by myself, so maybe I'm an introvert and that's the best kind of person to be an only child."

"Yeah. What were your parents like?"

"Distant. You were talking about having someone else raise your kid. I was one of those."

"Oh. I'm sorry."

"No. I guess what happens to you, it's just normal. Right? You don't know what it would be like to have been raised by your mom, and just daycare is the way your childhood went. I guess I don't recall ever being confused about who my mom was, but I do know sometimes I was sad when I left daycare and happy when I got to go back."

"Oh. That's terrible."

"Yeah. It wasn't that I liked daycare so much, it was just... It seemed happier there than in my home."

"Wow." She felt so bad for him. She couldn't imagine liking being somewhere other than her home. For her whole childhood, even school, which she loved, didn't compare to hanging out at the house with her siblings. Now, she was like every other kid, she supposed, and as she got older, her friends became more and more important, until she probably would have chosen her friends over her parents, but leaving for college had been hard, not because she was leaving her friends but because she was leaving her home and her family.

"What did your mom do?"

"She didn't work, she just didn't want to take care of me."

Her jaw dropped at that. She had known that there were kids out there with parents like that. Although, she didn't think a whole lot of them went to daycare. But she supposed there were some moms who sent their kids to daycare just so they could have a break from them.

"Wow."

He nodded. "I think parenting is hard. I don't really blame her, because I've seen parents who didn't want their kids, and the kids end up abused or neglected. So at least they sent me somewhere where I was going to be taken care of."

She felt her heart clench. He kind of justified everything as fine, and she didn't want to argue with him. After all, it was his experience, and he put the best possible spin on it. Far be it from her to try to tarnish that image. But it made her a little bit angry at his mom. For being so...selfish. Except, he was right. She knew that raising kids was hard. Her mom had mentioned more than once how often she had wanted a break, but she had grown up in New York and their dad had grown up in Florida, and they had compromised when they moved to Virginia when they got married.

She handed him the second string of lights, and he plugged it into the first and started stringing it without comment.

His fingers had brushed hers, and she turned from him, balling them up into a fist and just standing there, trying not to think about the fact that their fingers had brushed.

"Are you okay?" he said from behind her, putting a hand on her shoulder.

She startled and jumped, and his hand dropped.

"Sorry. I was lost in thought there for a minute."

"You don't need to get depressed about my childhood. It was okay. I mean, I think I'm okay now. I guess we're shaped by our childhood, and it sticks with us all of our life, better than so many other things, but we're not bound by it. If it wasn't good, we can overcome it. God says we can overcome anything through Him. So, don't be sad. It just gave me something that made me stronger. A trial that strengthened me."

"Yeah. You have such a great outlook on that," she said, taking a breath and trying to clear her mind from other thoughts. She just needed to remember that she couldn't touch him. That was a bad idea.

"So what made you decide to go to med school? You loved sewing up your brothers and sisters every time they needed it?"

"No. Honestly, all I wanted to do was come back and have a clinic here in town. I didn't even really think about being a doctor. It was just the idea. Which is weird, I know, but true."

"You must have had some aptitude for it. It's not like anybody can be a doctor."

"I think if you're willing to work hard enough, anybody can. Yeah, it takes a lot of studying, and if you're not naturally gifted, it's going to be really hard, at least the book learning stuff. All the Latin and drug names that you have to learn. And you're supposed to have all of that on the top of your head. And a lot of times, you don't have a whole lot of time to study because you're busy with rotation and all the other things that they make you do. But I was definitely not the smartest person there, and I was able to get through it."

He jerked his head but didn't say anything more. She didn't go into all the college classes and the science classes which were rather hard, but she knew a lot of med students who had needed tutoring and who would probably make really good doctors, once they got through the rigorous studies.

Chapter Twenty-Seven

Sometimes intelligence wasn't the only indicator of success. Although, Terry didn't want a doctor who didn't know what they were doing, and she supposed a few of those graduated as well, like in any field. It was just that doctors could be involved in life-and-death situations.

"All right, how's that?" Judd said, putting his hands on his hips and standing back so that he was beside her.

She didn't move over, and his elbow just barely missed her.

"You did a great job. They're so evenly placed."

"I told you I had drill sergeant training in putting Christmas lights up, so they ought to be pretty good."

"Did your mom hate Christmas?"

"She loved it. She decorated everything very tastefully, just so you know," he said, putting a hand out. "But everything. And usually she started at the end of October. And everything was up until the end of January."

"It sounds like she really did love it."

"I think she just loved...elegance. Or style or something. She didn't put a ton of things out, but they were all very...coordinated, I guess."

"She sounds like a complicated woman," Terry finally said. She wasn't quite sure how Judd actually felt about her.

"Yeah. I think she is. And I think it's hard for her to show her emotions. But she's very demanding too, which makes that even harder. If she showed a lot of love but demanded a high standard, I'd probably be a completely different person."

"I think I'd be very different. A child needs to be shown love." She said that very firmly and emphatically. She believed that with all her heart and was struck again at how blessed she was to grow up in the home that she had. There was never a dearth of love, whether her dad was home or not. Her mom more than made up for everything, laughing and having a good time, and making sure that all of her children were hugged and cared for to the best of her ability.

"All right, I guess we start the bulbs now," he said, pulling the box out that they had set aside earlier and opening it up. "My mom always said to put the big ones on the bottom and the little ones on the top."

"Interesting. I would have thought you should scatter them evenly all over the tree to make it look uniform."

"I don't know where she got that idea, but she was insistent upon it."

She figured he could probably tell her times where he had decorated something and his mom had completely redone it.

Instead, he got a bulb, which still had the hook attached, and looked at the tree. "Are you sure you don't care?"

"She marked you. You're scared you're going to put it in the wrong place."

"Maybe?"

"How about we just throw them on. See if the hooks hold them."

He gasped, but it was fake and exaggerated. "We might break something."

"And that was another fear?"

"Exactly. Everything was expensive, ordered from Europe or antique. Irreplaceable. I broke a couple of those and learned very quickly to be extremely, extraordinarily careful."

"I'm surprised she allowed you to touch them at all."

"She didn't really do it herself. Usually the housekeeper did it, or she even hired people, but there were a few years where she tried to get me to do it. Obviously I still have nightmares about it."

"I don't think that's how decorating is supposed to go at all." He was coming back for another ball, and she touched his arm, looking up at his face. Wishing that they could make new memories, happy memories. The kind of memories she wanted him to have. "Christmas must be terrible for you?"

He stopped when she touched him, and now he looked down at her with a little smile on his face.

"No. I told you. You can make it what you want to make it. God gave us the power to control our thoughts. And I decided I was going to do that. Now, I'm not saying it was easy, and I'm not saying that I don't have flashbacks, and obviously I still have those memories, since we spent the last hour talking about them, but..."

"I'm sorry. I didn't mean to make you talk about stuff that made you unhappy."

"No. I didn't mean that at all. I just know that I'm not over it. Completely. Maybe I never will be. You know? This whole life is a struggle. And our sin especially, but our actions and our attitudes affect other people, possibly for the rest of their lives. Maybe my mom didn't realize when she was being controlling and grumpy and unhappy, that it was going to affect me."

"And your memories of Christmas."

He lifted a shoulder. "Yeah."

"So you're making new ones."

"That's right. I don't allow myself the bad thoughts, don't think about the bad memories, don't dwell on them. I make my life what I want it to be."

If she were doing that, she would have more people in it. But he had said he was an introvert. And she could understand that a little bit. By the time she got home from her clinic, she was ready to relax and unwind, although she never minded doing that with him.

She squeezed his arm, and she didn't see him move, but suddenly his hand was lying on top of hers.

"This is a new memory. A good one." He smiled, looking down at her.

His arm under her hand, his hand on top of hers, and his whole face beaming down at her. It was tempting to step closer.

"It's a good one for me too," she said honestly.

"Jingle Bells" had been playing, but it morphed into a rendition of "O Holy Night," and the small beat of silence had them breaking apart and grabbing more bulbs.

It took another hour, but they finally had everything put on perfectly, including the unopened package of icicles that had been tucked away in his box.

"My mother hated these."

"Why? They're my favorite decoration."

"Mine too. They just shimmer and sparkle and make everything look beautiful, but she hated them because they constantly fell off the tree and got knocked around everywhere."

"I see. Because that's true. Seems like every time you walk by the tree, you get at least twenty attached to you, and there's always some on the floor."

"She would pick them up in July and complain that they were there and say she was never putting any on her trees again."

"When she packed the Christmas decorations away, she wanted them to stay away?"

"Exactly. I'm being kind of hard on her. Our house always looked beautiful. It was like a postcard. And I did enjoy looking at it. I mean, I'm a guy, so it wasn't like I sat around admiring it, but it was peaceful and pretty and garnered a lot of compliments from everyone who saw it."

"Ours always looked like six little kids had put the decorations up, which six little kids *had* put decorations up, so no wonder."

"Bet that was fun."

"It was."

Her hot chocolate was cold, but the air felt warm and cozy. They put the extra boxes away and then stood back and admired their handiwork.

"I think it looks gorgeous," she said, realizing that it had been years since she had had a full-size tree up in her living room like this.

"I agree. It could beat any one of my mom's," he said.

He put a hand around her, laying it on her shoulder which felt natural, and she leaned into him without thinking. With the snow falling outside, and the cozy heat of the house, and the pretty decorations, and the good companionship, she felt like she was glowing.

"I'll decorate a tree with you anytime. Not because you're such a great decorator, although you are," he squeezed her shoulder when she started to straighten, because she was going to call him on that one, "but because you're good company."

"So are you. And that's pretty admirable. I had a great example in my mom and an even better example, if possible, in my dad. And all I have to do is think about what they would do, and I have that laid out for me. You know? Like I can do the right thing, be the kind of person I want to be, when I think about how they did things. You don't have that."

"Maybe I just had to think about things a little harder, to decide what I wanted to be and do."

"You have. And you've done an admirable job." She looked up at him, smiling, and kind of turned to face him. His hand slipped off her shoulder and somehow ended up in her hair.

Her hand touched his waist, and she took that step that she had been longing to take.

Their eyes met and held, and she felt like she was standing on sunshine and holding her breath at the same time.

He leaned down a little, and she stretched up, and she was pretty sure it was all her when their lips touched.

He seemed a little surprised, and she almost pulled back, but his hand moved again, warm and solid around the back of her neck, as his other hand wrapped around her waist and pulled her even closer.

He tasted like hot chocolate and Christmas, and her thoughts of the little boy who had spent lonely days with the mother who was never satisfied evaporated as she pressed closer, never wanting that feeling to end.

And then, just as quickly as it happened, one of them pulled back, she wasn't sure which one, and they stared at each other. And she realized what she'd done.

What had she done? She hadn't meant to kiss him. How was this going to change everything? They had such a great thing going on, they were sharing a duplex, enjoying each other's company, treating the other with respect and kindness, and now... Did she want this? Did she really want to start a relationship with this man? Because that was what kissing was to her. It wasn't just a one and done. She didn't think he was the kind of man who acted like that, either, but maybe he was. And it was going to be very awkward for her because she wasn't. Not even a little bit.

"Good night," she said quickly and hurried from the room.

She didn't know why she was running away. That wasn't in her personality at all. She was a commanding personality, outgoing and friendly, facing things head-on, she couldn't have gotten to where she was if she didn't. But she didn't stop even when he called her name.

She was halfway up the steps when he called it again.

"Terry!"

She didn't stop until she was at the top, and then, with her hand on the banister, her head down, she said, "I'm sorry. I'm sorry."

"I'm not!" he said from the bottom of the stairs. "It was the best night of my life, and you made it better."

"Good night," she called, hurrying to the door, opening it quickly, and stepping in. She couldn't get it shut fast enough behind her, and she leaned against it.

What had she done?

She was still wondering the same thing four hours later as she lay in bed staring at the ceiling.

What had she been thinking?

She didn't do anything without thinking about it first, planning it, working toward it. She had everything thought out, and she worked according to her goals and the things she wanted to accomplish. She didn't just go around kissing random men.

She wasn't the kind of woman who kissed a guy and it meant nothing. It had meant everything to her, and she wasn't sure she wanted it to. Did she really want to start a relationship with Judd? And how did he feel about it? He had said that it was the best night of his life, but what did he think they were going to do now? Were they just going to be friends who kissed?

She shuddered at the thought. That wasn't who she was, and it wasn't who she wanted to be.

What were they going to do? How were they going to act? The thought made her cold.

A noise made her freeze.

It happened again. The creaking of the steps.

She noticed that the two middle steps creaked no matter how you went up or down them.

So that must be Judd, going downstairs.

Immediately she thought about the Secret Saint and how she hadn't pressed him for answers.

She had wanted to, but she hadn't been sure she wanted to know. Mostly because... There was a reason he was trying to keep things secret. The few people that she'd talked to who had actually been in contact with someone during the Secret Saint gift giving had said that they couldn't say.

Whoever it was was trying to keep it pretty quiet. And he'd been successful.

She slipped out of bed, still wide awake, still thinking that she might have made a big mistake, and padded over to the window, standing at the side and looking out.

Sure enough, shortly she heard the front door creaking just a bit. If she hadn't heard it a million times, she might not even notice what it was. And sometimes at night, she had music playing. But she didn't this evening. She'd left her speaker downstairs.

After she waited a few more minutes, Judd came into sight, hurrying down the sidewalk.

She hadn't asked him what he was doing this evening, but then she often didn't. And just assumed that he was going to bed and staying there. Sometimes she met him in the morning, but he had told her when she first moved in that he had odd hours, and she never really thought a whole lot about it. He'd mentioned that the courthouse needed to be cleaned overnight when there was no one there, and he had a key to get in.

She wished she would have pressed him about his plans for the night. Were there other jobs he did in the middle of the night?

She looked at the time, one o'clock in the morning. Did he clean the courthouse at this hour?

She went back to bed, but she didn't go to sleep easily.

Chapter Twenty-Eight

"That doesn't look too bad," Wilson said as he stared up at the enormous tree they had just put up in the town square.

"Actually, I think it looks pretty good," Judd said, standing back with his friend and looking at it.

He had just been standing looking at a tree with Wilson's sister a few hours ago.

He thought the tree that Terry and he had decorated was better, but he knew his opinion was biased.

This one was done pretty well, but without the icicles. They wouldn't last outside anyway. It was just lights and bulbs. It hadn't taken long at all.

Although, knowing about Wilson's past made him see Wilson in a slightly different light. It's funny that they had worked together for so long and Wilson had never mentioned it, and he spent one night with Terry, and he knew everything. Maybe not everything. But a lot.

And that kiss.

It had been amazing to him, such a huge, life-changing thing, but she had run.

It made him feel like he was a terrible kisser, which could absolutely be true.

Or maybe he just screwed something else up and didn't even realize it. It wasn't like he had done this a lot. In fact, he'd deliberately chosen not to do it a lot, because he didn't want to kiss someone that he wasn't planning on getting married to. It was too much like kissing another man's wife. Because eventually, she would be married to someone else, not him. He wouldn't want to see her on someone else's arm, knowing that he had kissed her. The thought made him slightly sick, mostly because he thought that God would not be pleased with actions like that.

Regardless, it might have come back to bite him, since obviously his kissing wasn't on Terry's list of things to enjoy.

"Hello? Judd?" Wilson slapped his shoulder and started walking away.

"Sorry." He figured that Wilson had said something to him, but he wasn't sure what it was.

"Didn't you hear me?" Wilson said as they walked along, with Judd realizing that there was a glow in the eastern sky.

"No, sorry. I was thinking."

"Don't get all sentimental about Christmas on me, Secret Saint." He laughed, and Judd smiled, but he didn't feel a whole lot like laughing.

What was he going to do now? He didn't think he was going to be able to just pretend that nothing happened tonight when she came home.

"I'll try not to," he said,

"Hurry home. You don't want anyone to see us."

Wilson got in his truck and drove away quickly, while Judd hurried down the sidewalk. Still wondering what he should do. Should he try to ignore it? Try to confront her with questions? What was he going to say, "Am I a terrible kisser? Is that why you ran?"

He didn't think he could utter those words, but he really did want to know. He was almost positive being a terrible kisser wasn't going to make her hate him. Maybe he'd rather he didn't know.

He didn't usually get this wrapped and twisted up with things, but it was Terry, and he had some pretty strong feelings for her. She was...pretty much perfect.

He didn't mean that literally. He knew she wasn't perfect. He knew she had faults and flaws and things that would probably drive him crazy, but they seemed to get along so well together, and he enjoyed her company, felt an attraction to her, but more than that, admired her love of God and family and her desire to serve and be a blessing.

He was still thinking about it when he reached his house and stepped inside.

He was so deep in thought that he had gone up two steps before he looked and realized that Terry stood at the top.

He ran through his mind, trying to figure out what he could say if she asked where he was. Which she was almost certainly going to do. She had one hand on her hip.

She was dressed like she was ready to go to the practice, but she didn't typically leave until a good bit later. In fact, he'd never run into her this early. It was only seven o'clock. Usually by eight, she was downstairs in the kitchen. They often drank coffee together, but they didn't talk a whole lot in the morning. She didn't seem to be a morning person. And he didn't care. He didn't talk a whole lot anytime, except with her.

"Good morning," he said, his voice measured and soft.

"Morning," she said, sounding very much like a queen talking to her subject. Only her voice was soft too. She had one eyebrow cocked, and her head tilted. "Where have you been?"

She asked like she deserved to know the answer, and he supposed maybe she did, since he had just kissed her last night.

Although, if he was thinking really hard about it, she was the one who kissed him. At least, she started it, although when he said that, he felt like he was about two years old and tattling to the teacher.

What was he going to say? The truth? She might hate him. He could ruin everything that he and Wilson had done if he told her where he really was. She might post it all over social media. He didn't think that she was like that, but he knew that sometimes when a woman got angry, she got a little unreasonable.

At least, going by his mom and the other women that he'd known growing up. He didn't think that Terry would be like that, but a lot of people didn't think his mom was like that either. They had a rude awakening.

"I was out," he said carefully, climbing up the stairs. He figured that if she let him touch her, maybe he could tell her the truth. Maybe that meant that everything was going to be okay. That she wasn't going to be mad at him or hate him. Or whatever else.

Her lips tightened a bit, and he figured that that probably wasn't the answer that she wanted. Could he tell her the truth? Should he keep quiet? It would help if he knew what was going on in her head with what happened last night.

"About last night," he began, but she cut him off.

"I have someone waiting for me at the clinic." Her eyes darted away, and she wouldn't look at him as she moved forward, waiting for him to move so she could go downstairs.

Tempted to stand there, to force her to talk to him about it and at least let him know if she didn't like him and was upset that it had happened, or... He wasn't even sure what other option there could be. Maybe he should just stop trying. He kissed her, she'd run away, now she didn't want to talk to him. He supposed he should just take a hint.

He nodded, moving ahead and shifting so she could go through.

But then he remembered that the parade was that evening.

"I just want to remind you that I'll leave supper on the stove. I have to have time to get the horses hitched up and at the starting point," he said, knowing that they were scheduled to ride together with Belle and Bob hitched to the wagon.

"Thank you. I told you I'm closing the clinic early, and I should be at the parade well before it starts." She paused on the step while she spoke, then he noticed her hand tightened on the railing before she continued down the stairs, grabbing her coat and hurrying outside.

Well, whatever she was feeling, she wasn't going to ditch him at the parade. Or at least she wasn't planning on it now, although whether that was how it ended up or not, he didn't know.

Chapter Twenty-Nine

*I*t came as no surprise to Terry when her patients came in and started talking about the Christmas tree that had been put up in the town square.

She knew immediately what Judd had been doing the previous night.

Why hadn't he told her? Didn't he trust her? Why did he feel like he needed to keep it a secret from her? Like he could kiss her, and that was fine, but he couldn't tell her he was the Secret Saint?

Although to be fair, she had kissed him.

She tried to focus on her work, but the excitement in the air was palpable, since almost everyone she saw was planning on going to the Christmas parade or else were going to be in it.

She had just finished up with a patient and was looking at her iPad to get the information on the next one when her nurse, Ashley, touched her arm and leaned in.

"There's someone in the waiting room who would like to see you," she said softly.

That was odd. It was the first time that had happened, and she immediately looked up, searching Ashley's face and trying to figure out what was going on.

"If it's an emergency—"

"You'll know when you see him. Just go talk to him."

Her eyes got big, but she clicked off her iPad and tried to orient herself before she hurried to the door.

The waiting room was empty, except for Judd, who was at the far end, standing beside a woman who sat with a small child in her lap.

His head came up as she came to the door.

She looked at him, then at the woman and child, and then hurried over, her brows drawn.

He met her halfway, meeting her gaze with an unwavering one of his own. She'd left without talking to him about last night and the kiss that they'd shared, which she'd run away from. And maybe he wondered why, but he had to know. Had to understand that he was so new and different and... That wasn't the way she usually was, and maybe he didn't understand.

She probably shouldn't assume that he understood that she just needed some time to process and didn't know what to say.

"This is Dana. Her daughter woke up this morning with a fever, and she didn't want to call, because she knew she couldn't pay. Whatever it costs, you can bill me."

He waited until she looked him in the eye and nodded, and maybe the knowledge of who he was showed on her face.

He pressed his lips together but didn't acknowledge that. "I have to leave. There are some things I need to do, but whatever it costs, her medicine, everything."

"Normally I send perscriptions to the pharmacy. So I technically am not involved in that part of it."

"Right. Of course." He ran a hand through his hair.

"But I just have the patients that are waiting in the exam rooms right now, and then I'll be taking a lunch break. I can...take her to the pharmacy and pay for it myself."

"I usually have cash set aside for this type of thing, but... I don't today. I'll pay you back," he said, his expression hopeful as he turned back toward her.

"We'll see what it is. I'll text you."

"Thanks. I might be out of service, but I'll respond as soon as I can."

Where was he going that he would be out of service? And why was she constantly wondering what he was doing? What did it matter to her?

Except she knew it did, because she cared about him. A lot. When a person cared about someone else, they wanted to know.

She nodded, and he started to walk away, then he touched her arm. With a glance over his shoulder at the woman who held her small daughter tight, he lowered his voice even further and leaned down. "I'm sorry about last night. I didn't mean to upset you."

She could hear him swallow, and then he moved around her and walked out the door.

He apologized, when it was her fault. She appreciated the fact that he was willing to be humble, to take the blame, to try to move them past this, and she gave him all the credit in the world for that. But she couldn't allow him to do that, when it was her fault.

She wanted to grab him and stop him, but there was a worried mother with a sick child in front of her, and she had more people to see back in the exam rooms.

"Hello, Dana. All of my rooms are full right now, but the nurse will bring you back as soon as she can, and we're going to get your daughter fixed up, okay?"

She nodded, looking relieved.

Terry walked back, knowing that she probably was not going to get a lunch break today, or she was probably going to be running around on it, but she wouldn't change it for anything. She would have to thank Judd for bringing the woman, because it felt good to be able to help someone who needed it. And then she and Judd were going to have to talk. She was pretty sure he wanted to, and she needed it. But first, they had a parade to get through.

Chapter Thirty

*J*udd stood beside Belle's head, slowly stroking her forehead between her wise old eyes.

Belle didn't seem to be the slightest bit bothered by all the hoopla that was going on around them. Bands warmed up, people threw batons and balls, kids yelled, and fire truck engines rumbled.

It was a symphony of noises that the horse didn't usually experience, but she was taking it all in stride.

Bob, on the other side of her, was doing just fine as well. He thought they would be okay. They hadn't given him a single minute of trouble when he had been picking up kids and dropping them off at church on Sundays.

They had decided to put all the kids that they normally picked up for church in the back of the wagon to ride in the parade. Wilson and he had gone and gotten way more candy than either one of them thought was necessary, and all the kids would have some to throw as they went along the parade route.

Amy and Jones were going to supervise the kids and make sure they didn't use their candy as weapons and people as targets.

Or whatever else a child could think of, which, in Judd's experience, was way more than he ever could.

And Terry was going to ride beside him.

Terry had been fine with the plan, and when they'd been talking about it, she had even said that she didn't need to go along, but Amy had insisted.

There had been some kind of silent communication or at least some long, thoughtful looks that Terry had given her sister.

Personally, Judd thought that Amy and Jones were already in love with each other and didn't realize it. But he wasn't exactly an expert on that kind of thing and certainly hadn't told anyone. Although, if he and Terry were talking, that might have been the kind of thing that he might have told her.

He looked around again, hearing the laughter of the children in the back and knowing that the parade had already started. They were waiting their turn in line. He hoped that Terry was able to get around the traffic.

He also hoped that she wasn't going to give him the silent treatment all night. He supposed he didn't need any explanation as to why she ran away from him, and if she didn't want to talk about it and just wanted to pretend it never happened, he was okay with that. But he hated that things now felt stilted between them. Like in the waiting room today. He'd...touched her arm, and she hadn't shrunk back, but it felt like maybe he shouldn't have. And they just didn't have their...easiness between them, he didn't even know what to call it, but he missed it. If he did know what to call it, though, he certainly couldn't find the words to figure out how to tell her that he wanted it back.

"They're beautiful. Even more beautiful up close," Terry said as she arrived at his side from the opposite direction that he was looking.

"They're a good team. And they work well together. Sometimes you get horses together, and it's like they're pulling against each other, but Belle's the one that's willing to work, and Bob kind of drags in his harness, but she snaps him right to it, and they end up being really good."

"I see. It's the girl who needs to keep the guy in line," Terry said, and her sparkling eyes were back. Did that mean that she wasn't angry at him anymore?

He didn't want to ask her and ruin whatever it was between them, and he had just thought to himself that he was going to let it go...

"You're not mad at me anymore?"

Her eyes got big, and her mouth formed an O.

"I wasn't angry at you," she said, glancing around. "I was just... surprised. I kissed you. I don't know why you were apologizing."

"Because I let it happen?" He wasn't sure why either, just he figured he had done something, and he hadn't meant to. Whatever it was, he wouldn't do it again if she would just tell him.

"No. I'm certainly not going to get mad at you because I kissed you and you allowed it to happen." She looked up at him, lifting her brows, waiting until he acknowledged her words with a nod. "Also, thank you for supper. It was delicious."

"You're welcome. I was happy to be able to do it for you. You had a big day."

"You always act like doing kind things for me is a privilege for you." She laughed and rolled her eyes. "You're a kind man."

That made him feel good, but he wasn't sure whether that was a straight arm or not. He wasn't thinking that had anything to do with romance or the way he felt about her.

"I just wanted to make sure that the horses were not going to go crazy when all of the noise started. That's why I'm standing here at Belle's head. Making sure she settles down. But I think we can safely go get on the wagon seat now."

"All right. Also, I thought the tree that you put up in the town square looks really nice," she said as she gave him a last look and then moved to her side of the wagon.

He stood staring at her. So she knew. Had someone told her? Or had she figured it out?

He followed her around, holding a hand out to give her help. "Did someone tell you? Or did you figure it out?"

"We need to talk, but we probably ought to get through this evening first." She lifted her brows, as though asking whether he would be willing to talk or not. Of course. He wasn't much of a talker, and he didn't always enjoy digging through every emotion he ever had, but he genuinely wanted to try to work things out with her. However that looked.

It was encouraging that she wanted it too. Although, he told himself to calm down. She wasn't saying she wanted to work things out. She was just saying she wanted to talk. Maybe she wanted to explain why she didn't want to be with him. That was a possibility too. One he couldn't discount.

"Is it time to go yet?" one of the kids yelled as he climbed up on the seat.

"I can't go any faster than the people in front of me," he said, nodding at the fire truck that was right in front of him.

Hopefully it didn't honk its horn, although he was pretty sure that his horses would be okay with it. Still, after they started, he would be careful to keep a good bit of distance between himself and the truck.

"Does everybody have their candy?" Amy said in a loud, cheerful voice.

"If you need some more, I've got plenty, and we're not keeping any until next year, so make sure you throw it all out today," Jones said, holding up a big bag of candy.

Amy and Jones's eyes met, and Judd turned back around. They had everything well in hand.

"Is this your first parade?" Terry asked as she sat beside him.

"It is. You?"

"No. I was in the band in high school. I played in a ton of parades, and I rode in a float in the homecoming parade, but this is my first time on a horse-drawn wagon."

He remembered the homecoming parade now that she mentioned it. She had been beautiful that night, and even though he knew that he would never be with her, he had admired her as she'd gone by.

She had been with someone else, the student council president or something like that. He couldn't remember. But he admired beauty, and to him, Terry was the epitome of beauty.

"Do you want to drive?" he asked as the fire truck ahead of them slowly started out.

"Are you serious?" she asked, sounding shocked.

He nodded his head, then looked over his shoulder. "I'd better start out, so I don't lose anyone out the back." Even though the endgate was closed, he didn't want anyone tumbling. "As soon as I get them going, there shouldn't be too much to driving them. They'll just go straight unless we guide them one way or the other. Of course, sometimes they get off-kilter a bit. But I've been driving them around, so I don't think they're going to have too much push and pull in them."

"You mean Belle already has Bob in line?" she asked, and then she said, "Are their names from the line 'bells on bobtails ring'?"

He laughed. "Yeah. It took a little bit, but she got there."

"Oh goodness, that's not exactly obvious," she said, looking at the horses and shaking her head. Her laughter was easy, and that made him feel better.

"You know, I saw you ride in the homecoming parade. You're beautiful."

That felt a little random, but it had been in his head since she mentioned it, though maybe he should have just kept his mouth closed.

"I have better company tonight," she said, and she looked him in the eye, and as her words penetrated, his heart started to smile.

"Belle and Bob are pretty nice horses," he said, grinning.

"They are, and you're a pretty nice guy."

He did not want nice. Nice was not good. Nice was not what he was aiming for. Okay, nice was good, it just wasn't his goal.

But he couldn't make her feel something she didn't. So, he just tried to be himself.

"It's too bad you can't enter the hot chocolate contest. The hot chocolate that you made while we were decorating the Christmas tree was really good."

"It was mostly a mix. I always add a couple of Hershey's Kisses if I have them in the cupboard. That's all that makes it different."

"Wow. I knew there was something unique about it, but we were doing so many other things that I never thought to say anything."

"Now you know my secret."

"What are you doing for Christmas?" she asked.

"I don't know," he said. "I suppose it probably depends on you."

"Me?"

A muscle twitched in his cheek, and he tried to relax. "I don't typically kiss girls and then walk away from them. If I look like that kinda guy, I'm sorry. But yeah. I'd like to be with you on Christmas. But I don't know how you feel about it."

They had reached the edge of the crowd and parade route, and the kids had started to throw candy.

"Someone's waving at you." She nodded toward the other side of the street.

He looked over and nodded his head at a little girl who had her hand up and was waving for all she was worth.

"I think she's waving at you," he said, giving Terry a look.

"All right," Terry said, lifting her hand up and waving.

"I'm going to my mom's, and I was wondering if you wanted to come with me?" she said as she waved to a few people on the other side, not looking at him.

"Yes." That was an easy answer. No matter what she said to him tonight, whether she decided that kissing him was a mistake and she didn't want to do it again, he still wanted to be with her. That hadn't changed. He didn't think it probably would, not for a long time, if ever. He wasn't the kind of guy who fell in love with a whole pile of different women. After all, it had taken him thirty years to find this one, and everything in him said that she was the exact right one.

"I want a whole bunch of children. Like, ten," she said, laughing at some kids along the road as they scrambled for the candy that was being thrown.

"Same. I don't want any child to have to grow up by themselves. They should have siblings."

She paused, looking at him. "You would know."

He wasn't sure why they were talking about this. But she could just take the lead and go where she wanted.

"Dana's daughter had an ear infection, and it looked like the beginning of strep throat. I gave her some samples of medication that I had in the office, and then we went to the pharmacy and I filled her prescription for her after I took a culture."

"Thanks for taking care of that."

"You do that a lot?"

"I told you. Typically I have cash that I give to people, but I'd used it for something else and hadn't gotten anything else out. I didn't have time today."

"Because you are too busy doing your other good deeds?"

"Who told you?" he asked instead of answering her.

"You keep being evasive. It makes me feel like I can't trust you."

That brought him up short. He didn't want her to wonder where he was or what he was doing because she thought he might be doing something with someone else.

"I'm not in this by myself, and I don't want the person who's doing it with me to be outed even though I was. You know?"

"So someone else is funding you?" Terry said, keeping her voice down so it didn't travel to the back of the wagon.

"No."

Her eyes narrowed, and then someone caught her eye across the street and she smiled and waved. "You're doing it yourself? Paying for it yourself?"

"Yeah. I am."

"And I'm supposed to believe that? But I've been here. I've seen you. You're not working full time. You're just doing odd jobs."

"Not everything is the way it seems, is it?"

He knew this wasn't the best place for them to be having this discussion, but the idea that she didn't trust him bothered him. It hadn't occurred to him that that was the way she was feeling.

And he wanted to tell her everything. Let her know anything she wanted so that he was an open book. Because he could be.

"I'm not doing anything wrong. Morally or...to you. It bothers me that you said you couldn't trust me. I promise you, I don't know how to handle one girl, let alone more."

"Sometimes I don't think men realize that being too kind to too many women makes the one that they're interested in feel like she's not special."

His mouth opened, and then it closed. He wasn't quite sure what she was saying.

"I'm interested in you, and it's important to me that you know that you're special. Because there isn't anyone else." He huffed out a breath and looked between Belle's ears for a moment. "There really never has been."

"I wondered. I don't really remember you too much in high school, but I don't remember you being part of a couple."

"I wasn't." Mostly because no one was interested in him, and even back then, he had known that he didn't want to date around.

"So I guess that if you think a girl is special, you won't keep secrets from her."

"I wasn't sure where we were. That...kiss took me by surprise. Not that I didn't want it," he said, turning to face her fully so that she would see how sincere he was. He had dreamed about that kiss. But she ran away. "I couldn't share any secrets if you're not willing to talk to me."

"Yeah. You're right. I guess I was blaming you, when I should have been looking at myself."

"No. It's not my desire to make you feel bad."

"The truth shouldn't make me feel bad. And if it does, it's not your fault," she said, smiling and waving over his shoulder.

The bells on the horses' harness made a cheerful sound that filled the silence as they rode without speaking for a bit. They were more than halfway through the parade, and thankfully the hot chocolate competition booth would be at the end of the line, and he'd already scoped it out. There was a place where he could tie the horses until he was ready to go back to the trailer where he'd unloaded them.

"I don't regret the kiss either," she said softly.

He smiled. That was really all he needed to know.

"I had an uncle who wasn't rich, but he had a nice nest egg that he'd gotten from investing over time. When he died, he left me his money." He wasn't sure what to say about his parents, and then he figured he just might as well throw it out there. She wanted the truth. She didn't want secrets. And he thought that was right. He shouldn't be holding anything from her, if they were truly interested in each other, and he didn't think that she was any more inclined to have a superficial relationship than he was.

Maybe he should mention that first.

"I haven't had a whole lot of relationships, because I have a tendency to be serious. I don't go into them thinking it's just going to be a good time. I go into them thinking that this could be my life partner."

"I love that. It's my philosophy too. And probably the reason that I didn't date a whole lot in med school. There was a lot of getting together and breaking up, and I don't want to do that."

That was all he needed to hear. "My parents are rich. They own one of the big horse farms on the way down to Whisker Hollow. But my money isn't coming from them. It's from the inheritance I had. Even though they'd like for me to be in their business, it's just not something I've ever been interested in. I...have always wanted to do what I'm doing right now. Helping people, working when I can, and...not having the whole life of pressure, meetings, phone calls, emergencies that need to be addressed on a daily basis. That's just not me."

"You inherited money, and instead of spending it on yourself, you're using it to...help others?"

He nodded. "I get a monthly amount from the funds I have set up, and I spend it all if I can."

"Wow. How much?"

It wasn't a small sum, and when he named it, she stiffened and looked at him in shock. "That's more than my clinic should make in a month."

"You have expenses related to your clinic. I don't have anything but taxes, and the number that I just gave you is with the taxes taken out."

"Wow." She sighed, sounding sad, and looked away.

"What?" he asked, scared that he'd said something that bothered her. Did she think that he should be living in a mansion on a hill?

"I...wasn't really looking for someone who is rich."

"Are you serious? You're going to discriminate against me because I have money?"

"I don't know. Money destroys people."

"But you just said that you would have as much as I do on a monthly basis."

"True." She nodded. "I'm sorry. It just changes the whole way I think about you. I thought you were...poor, and that is fine. It didn't bother me at all, but now everything is shifting. You come from money."

"Yeah." The fire truck in front of them turned off as they reached the end of the street, and it went up the block to go down a backstreet and head to the fire station.

"There's our booth," she said. "It looks like folks are already in their places making hot chocolate."

"That was the point, I think. To have folks be able to get hot chocolate at the end of the parade. Just you and I are supposed to be in our booth, and we'll get a sample from everyone, taste them, and pick a winner."

"All the pressure," she said, smiling.

"I don't know. People get pretty serious about their hot chocolate around here."

"When you live in a town called Mistletoe Meadows, I think you do need to be serious about hot chocolate, and Christmas, and Secret Saints."

His head swiveled to hers, and he saw she was smiling, maybe teasing a little, and he thought that everything was okay.

Chapter Thirty-One

"And the winner is," Robert Galigher, mayor of Mistletoe Meadows and currently standing on the makeshift platform beside the hot chocolate competition, held up a cup of hot chocolate and said, "Geraldine McVey."

The crowd cheered, and Geraldine grinned from ear to ear.

Mr. Galigher waited for the applause to die down before he said, "And here is your trophy. Rather than some useless thing you're going to put on a shelf and have to dust every week or so, we had custom mugs made, with Mistletoe Meadows's name on it and the year and announcing you're a hot chocolate contest winner. You get a pair of them, so you can enjoy hot chocolate with your significant other."

She came to the booth, and he handed her the mugs. "You also get a gift card that's good at any store in Mistletoe Meadows." The second and third place winners had already been named and had gotten their prizes. "Now, if you'd like to taste the winning hot chocolate, go to her booth and buy yourself a mug."

The crowd cheered again, and Mr. Galigher said, "I'd like to thank the judges for their time and expertise."

Judd grinned. His only expertise was that he loved hot chocolate, but that seemed to be the only thing that was necessary.

"And I'd like to thank all the volunteers for their time and efforts today. They erected these little huts in record time, put the tables up, and had everything ready to go. We wouldn't be able to have this without them. Let's give them all a hand."

Judd leaned down to Terry's ear. "This is where I was today."

"Getting things ready for the parade?"

He nodded. "Along with Dana and her daughter, and going over the mountain to get candy for the kids to throw."

"Is that it?"

"And the tree. I did the tree this morning."

"I saw some pine needles on your coat and could smell it when you walked in. I figured what you'd been doing when I heard in my practice that it had been done. I understand why you didn't tell me, but I did feel like you didn't trust me."

"I can't tell everyone, otherwise it wouldn't be a secret. And there's enough people who know, like Dana, today. I didn't have enough time to get someone else to do it for me. And usually I have some lines that I use, and cash I can give, but I needed to talk to you, since I couldn't pay for it without making a trip to the bank, and I didn't have time."

She nodded. "I'm sorry I pressured you. But I didn't understand."

"Thank you guys for judging. You did an excellent job. I know it was a sacrifice." The mayor came over and slapped his hand on their shoulders.

"It was actually really hard. There was so much good hot chocolate, it was tough to make a choice."

"Yeah. You probably had to taste a couple three or four times to really make a good decision," he said, totally joking with them.

They just smiled, and he moved away as his phone buzzed.

I'll take care of the horses and wagon.

He glanced up to see Terry looking at him as he wrote OK and hit send.

"Wilson is going to take care of the horses and wagon."

"Oh, that's nice of him."

"Are you ready to go home?" Judd asked Terry. "Or would you like to walk around some?"

There were a few other booths set up, vendors that were selling things like freshly made doughnuts and cinnamon buns, and there was even someone selling Christmas cookies and funnel cakes.

"I'd like to go home," she said, and it made his heart smile to think that she might be eager to talk to him. Although, talking wasn't the only thing he was hoping for.

They turned up the sidewalk, and to his surprise, her fingers slid around his.

He looked down and then looked at her. She was smiling up at him, her eyes glowing.

He thought that was probably a really good sign and curled his hand around hers, cradling it and squeezing.

Loving the feel of her beside him and hoping that this was the start of something that lasted for a very long time.

They reached the porch, and the Christmas tree that they put up the day before shone happily in the window. It had been a long time since he'd come home to the happy lights of a Christmas tree and the warmth and welcome that it gave.

He saw that she had also hung a wreath on their door.

"I like it," he said as he opened it.

"They were selling them on the sidewalk as I walked home, and I couldn't resist."

"I would have hung it up for you if you'd have said something."

"I know, but it came with a hook, and there already was a nail on the door, so it wasn't hard."

He liked the little touches that she made to make their house welcoming.

They walked in, and he said, "I'd suggest we make some hot chocolate, but..."

"I think I've had my fill of hot chocolate for...today. I want to say for the season, but I think I'll be ready for more tomorrow."

"That's exactly how I feel. Let's wait until tomorrow and see how it goes."

They laughed together, and then she said, "I have a confession to make."

"Yeah?" He paused in the act of hanging up his hat. He had had to let go of her hand and had been hurrying, because he wanted to take it back.

She looked serious though, and his heart fell. What was she going to admit to?

"Today when I came home, the door to your living room was cracked."

"I guess I didn't get it shut tight when I left. I was kind of in a hurry."

"So I peeked in."

He was quiet. Knowing what she would have seen when she looked.

"I couldn't quite see anything, so...I pushed the door open a little wider." She pressed her lips together. "That's what I was apologizing for. It was one thing for you to let me in and for me to see, but I pushed it so I could see. The crack was a good two inches wide. I saw..."

"All the gifts and wrapping paper and stuff that I have on the floor for the Secret Saint things that I do."

"Yeah, that."

"You already know it's me. I can hardly be upset about it, especially since I left the door cracked."

"But I snooped. I...didn't really mean to, but I shouldn't have. It was wrong, and I'm sorry."

"No. You're right. If I want to be more, if you are special to me, there shouldn't be any secrets between us. You're welcome to look wherever you want to. You're welcome to see whatever you want to see. I'm an open book, except... I can't be to the town."

"I know. I understand now. I'm sorry I pushed you."

"I'm glad you did. It made me feel like you care."

"I do. I wasn't expecting to. This is surprising to me," she said, twisting her fingers a bit, before deliberately unhooking them and putting them down at her sides.

"Terry," he said, his fingers coming up and tracing down her cheek.

"Yeah?"

"It's surprising to me too. But not in a bad way. I... I've always admired you, and you're right, I didn't expect to fall for you. But..."

Was it too much? He couldn't really stop the words as they started to come out. "I love you. I think I've been falling in love with you since the day you first walked in and I showed you around the house. I couldn't think of anything to say, because I was a little overwhelmed. You were so compelling to me. I just felt a pull toward you."

"That's me! That's how I've been feeling. I keep thinking about this weird attraction, and I didn't want to label it attraction, but it's there, along with admiration for what you do, for your character, for the compassion that you show the people in the community. I have to say, it's inspiring."

"You don't think I'm lazy because I don't have a job?" he said, because he knew how the town talked. He knew that was how they thought about him. Some of them anyway.

"Mrs. Tucker gave me a lecture. And it made me realize that maybe you've chosen something that not a whole lot of people think is a good idea, but maybe the world would be better off if more people chose that way."

"Thanks. I don't know about that, but I just know that I wanted to do something different than what I saw growing up, but wanting and doing are two different things. You know? You have to make deliberate choices every day to be the person that you want to be, because it's so easy to get sidetracked."

"That's the way it is as a Christian too. You have to set boundaries for yourself and then not cross them. Otherwise, you end up doing a whole lot of things that you didn't plan on, just because you didn't take the time to make the choices that would take you in the direction that you want to go."

"I agree completely, life's like that. But I feel like being here with you is the right choice. I know we talked about this a bit on the wagon, but I'm not doing this lightly. I see us together for the rest of our lives." That was crazy. Nobody said that. It was too soon. He opened his mouth. "I know that's scary. That's probably such a weird thing to say—"

"No. I don't need to see more. I see that you're a good man, I see that you have integrity and character. I see that you keep your word. Maybe you don't know me as well, but I am perfectly comfortable with the idea of thinking about forever."

"I don't need to see more. I've known you all my life. And I love just the fact that you came back to your hometown and opened a clinic where you knew you weren't going to be making the big money that you could have made somewhere else, just because you wanted to be near your family. That says everything I need to hear."

She smiled, and they stared at each other for a moment.

"So, is tonight my night to kiss you first?" he asked, grinning a little, because she hadn't given him a choice yesterday.

"Are you asking for permission?" she asked, tilting her head a little and stepping closer.

"Yes. I'm asking for permission." And if she said no, he wouldn't be fine, but he would definitely listen to her. "If you think I'm moving too fast, it's okay."

"No. I was just laughing because I didn't ask permission yesterday, and I thought maybe you were asking because you were afraid I was just going to grab you and kiss you and you wanted to get a jump on me."

"I feel like I'm going to have to be pretty fast if I want to stay ahead of you."

"I'll let you lead," she said easily, and he could see in her eyes that she knew she could lead if she wanted to, but she was giving the privilege to him. If it was a privilege. It felt like a responsibility. And maybe a heavy one, since it was one thing to get oneself off track, it was a completely different thing to lead someone else the wrong way.

But kissing Terry was definitely not the wrong thing.

He lowered his head, and her hands slipped around his shoulders, and he pulled her closer, kissing her the way he'd wanted to for a long time.

And that time when he lifted his head, she didn't run away.

"I like the ending of this one better," he said after a moment of them staring at each other and maybe getting used to the idea of their new normal.

For him, he was thinking about lowering his head and doing it all again.

"I think I like the ending of this one better, too. Perhaps we should have an encore."

He grinned. "I was thinking the same thing."

And he lowered his head again.

JOIN JESSIE'S list and be the first to know about new releases and sales on her books!

READ ICICLE DREAMS, the next book in the Mistletoe Meadows series featuring Amy and Jones, best friends who decide to tie the knot for a hefty inheritance. Will a marriage of convenience destroy their lifelong friendship?

Sneak Peek of Icicle Dreams

*A*my McBride scooped dog food out of the bin. She tried not to sigh at the sight of the bottom of the bin as she picked her scoop up.

There was enough left for maybe two days. Three, if the two dogs that were being boarded went home today. And if she was very, very careful.

Dog food had increased in price dramatically over the last four years, and she did not have enough money in her account for even one bag.

All she had in her own cupboard were dried beans and a few bags of rice along with some pasta and some cans of tomatoes. She didn't even have sauce.

Lord, I know I'm not supposed to worry, but I feel like You're cutting it a little close.

Immediately she felt bad. Her tone was not humble or respectful.

I'm sorry, Lord. You know best. If I'm supposed to keep these dogs, You need to provide for them. And if I'm not, please help me to figure out what to do with them before we all starve.

There. That was a little better. She really did believe God was in control and that God planned things, and she absolutely believed with all of her heart and soul that God had wanted her to open up this pet sanctuary.

But when they had lost the Richmond Rebel sponsorship because she had trained someone who opened a pet sanctuary closer to their garage, she'd been struggling.

She didn't regret training Nolita to open up her own place, and she didn't begrudge Nolita the funding that came with the Richmond Rebels. In fact, Blade Truax, one of the brothers who owned the garage, had specifically talked to her about it. She had told him it was fine. She had wanted Nolita to have as much funding as possible and the best chance of success. She didn't want to be selfish.

But looking back, she wished she would have been just a little bit selfish. Although she figured even with the funding, Nolita was probably struggling the same way she typically did. There were so many animals and only so much money to go around.

Mocha shoved her nose through the wires as Amy poured dog food in the automatic feeder.

None of the automatic feeders were full. She was just putting in enough for one daily ration. She had checked the rations carefully and measured them out just as carefully. She wasn't going to give one ounce more than what she had to, but she wanted all the dogs to have what they needed.

"You're a sweetheart," she said to Mocha. The little dog was so affectionate. Even though her food was ready for her to eat, and she hadn't had anything extra in days, she still wanted to stay and have Amy pet her. She was some kind of terrier mixed with a large breed dog, which made her about fifty pounds, and all sweetness and affection. Mocha would make an amazing house pet for someone, but typically around the holidays, pet adoptions went down.

"You'll probably spend Christmas with me, which...it's not so bad, is it?" she asked, knowing that while she'd spend some time with the dogs, she'd also be with her family, her mom and her five siblings. They were all supposed to be in for Christmas, and there might even be some extra since she was fairly certain that her sister Terry would be bringing her... She didn't say that he was her boyfriend, but Judd was going to have that title, or even fiancé, soon.

She smiled, the idea of Terry being happy making her happy. Terry had been an example to her all throughout her life. Growing up, she could look to Terry to know what she should do. Humans were hardwired to have examples to look at and to emulate, to follow. So many of her classmates followed whatever it was on their TV, but Amy had been blessed. She had Terry.

Moving to the next dog, she scooped out of the bucket she carried and measured carefully.

Boomer came to the wire and stuck his nose through, waiting anxiously for his breakfast.

"Hey, Boomer. What's going on with you this morning?" she said as she scratched his ears while she poured the food in his automatic feeder.

He whined, and instead of going right over to his food like he typically did, he licked her hand.

The action made tears prick her eyes. He was so trusting. It was almost like he could tell that there was something on her mind. Something she worried about, and he wanted to make it better.

"I'm just going to trust God, Boomer. It's going to be okay."

She knew her words were true, but she also figured that if dogs could sense anxiety, they were probably sensing it in her right now. As much as she was trying to have faith and trust that God would take care of everything.

The dog licked her hand one more time and whined before going over and starting to eat his food.

She blinked back tears. She would figure something out. She had already been working part-time in her friend Jones's veterinary clinic. She manned the desk when he needed it and worked with him as a vet tech, either on farm calls or in his practice. He was mostly a small animal vet, but when a farmer around Mistletoe Meadows called an emergency, Jones did not turn them down.

His practice was not big. His "clinic" was in an elderly couple's garage, and he lived over the top. It was very unassuming, but that was Jones. He wanted to get his school bills paid off and a clientele established before he got his own building and sank a bunch of money into it.

She thought that was smart, and she knew that he was using everything that he made to try to pay his bills back after paying rent.

Regardless, she hadn't made enough to supplement what she lost when she lost the funding, and she was slowly sinking down into the red to the point where she was going to have to close. Or do something drastic; she wasn't sure what.

She emptied the last of the food in the bucket into the next dog's feeder and went back to fill up the bucket again. As she scraped the dog food from the bottom of the barrel, she thought about Elisha and the widow with the cruse of oil.

Was this how she felt? Almost running out, only it wasn't animals that were going to die with her, it was her son. That had to be worse.

Amy knew that she could always move in with her mom, but her mom already had her brother Gilbert, whose wife was dying of cancer, and their three children living there, and her younger sister Isadora was possibly moving in as well. Her husband had decided that he didn't love her anymore and had found someone else, and had left. He had not been kind when he had done it, and Isadora, who had been a stay-at-home mom, had been crushed.

Amy had wanted to go and strangle her ex, but obviously that wasn't the Christian thing to do. Still, it made her mad that someone could say vows, have a family, set up a home, and then just decide they didn't want to anymore.

That showed such a lack of character. Such a lack of decency. She just didn't understand it.

Well, in a way she did. She understood that human desires often affected human decisions. It was true for her.

Maybe that was why she was struggling so much. Maybe it hadn't been God's will for her to open this after all. Maybe she had just desired it so much that she had superimposed what she wanted as God's will.

She'd seen people do that, excuse their sin, saying it was God's will. She'd even seen a man, an assistant pastor, who cheated on his wife and left her and said that the woman that he left her for was God's will for him.

Her jaw dropped open when she heard that, but how did she argue with someone who was blind? She could point out black-and-white in the Bible that adultery was wrong. That breaking his word was wrong. That lying was wrong. Making promises that he didn't keep was wrong. That a man was supposed to provide for his family. And to not do so was wrong.

She just didn't understand it. At least she hadn't sinned, to her knowledge, in opening her pet sanctuary.

Just because things are hard, it doesn't mean you should doubt God.

Wow. That was the thought that she needed. It was funny how those things popped into her head at the most random times. Things she might have heard in a sermon or read in the Bible, and then, when she most needed them, they popped into her mind, or she should probably give credit where it was due and say that God brought it to mind.

Carrying the bucket back, hunching her shoulders against the cold December wind, she walked back to the shelter where the front pens were. Each pen had an outside run, and all of those would need to be cleaned this morning as well.

At least it wasn't below freezing. Where the dog poop froze before she could get it off the ground and then it just piled up until the ground finally unfroze and she had a huge mess.

Rain made things muddy and messy as well, and she was thankful that it was just cold and not miserable.

"Here you go, Alice. You thought I forgot about you." She dumped dog food into Alice's pan and patted the furry head before walking on.

Her brother Wilson and his friend, her sister's almost-boyfriend, had just put up a whole side of new pens for her. She already had dogs in them, two of which were boarders, and she would be getting money for their stay, thankfully. It couldn't come soon enough.

If you just told someone, you know a lot of people who would love to help you.

She sighed as she petted another wet nose and scooped more dog food out.

She didn't want to burden her friends and family even more. When she lost the funding, she'd mentioned to them that she wasn't going to have enough to make ends meet every month, and she'd been surprised at the people who had stepped up. That was why she had been able to go for a whole year without running out of money, and she was grateful to them, but she didn't want to keep asking them to bail her out. Her family and friends would start running as soon as they saw her coming.

Of course, she would do that before she would let any animal starve.

She set the bucket down and reached under her sweatshirt for the belt that she had started wearing.

Her pants had gotten so that they hung on her, and it was cheaper to dig a belt out of her closet than it was to buy a new wardrobe of clothes that would actually fit.

She tightened the belt one last notch—the last notch on the belt.

Her pants gathered together and felt uncomfortable, but she would rather be uncomfortable in her clothes and have more dog food. So she shoved the end of the belt back in the loops and pulled her sweatshirt down.

There. That felt a little better.

As she finished feeding the last of the dogs, she heard a noise before barking erupted, and she looked up, seeing a blue midsize pickup coming down her short drive.

Jones. He often came to help her before he opened his clinic, and the sight of him always made her heart happy. They'd been best friends forever, and he knew of her financial struggles, although he didn't know how desperate her situation was. She'd been getting up earlier so that she could have the animals fed before he came, so he wouldn't see the barrel of food and know that she was almost out. He'd help her. She knew he would. He had before. But she was tired of being a drain on every person who knew her.

Lord, help me know what to do. Should I tell my friends and family how desperate it is? It's close to Christmas, and I know money is tight. I don't want to burden anyone.

Jones pulled in, and she stood, holding the shovel, and waited for him to get out of his truck and walk over to her. He held two steaming cups of coffee, and her heart swelled, grateful that she'd somehow been blessed with such a great friend.

"It's chilly out this morning," Jones said, handing her a mug. It didn't matter which one, since they both took their coffee exactly the same—black.

"You are amazing," she said, lifting her brows and meeting his gaze before she took the mug, blowing a little on the top and taking a hot, burning sip. It warmed her the whole way to her stomach, and she sighed. "Thank you."

"You act like I've never done this before. When I literally do it every single morning."

"I am grateful, every single morning," she said, leaning the shovel against the end of the pole building and wrapping both hands around the mug.

"You should have gloves on," he said, seeing her bare fingers. He laughed and held up a hand. "But, I know, you wouldn't be able to pet the dogs as well if you wore gloves, you couldn't feel them, and they couldn't lick your hand. You'd miss all that stuff, and..." He stopped, and his expression said, *did I miss anything?*

"You're right. Sometimes I wear gloves though," she said, in her defense, although there really wasn't much of a defense. How could she defend herself? It was chilly, her hands were freezing, and the coffee mug felt amazing. She wouldn't need it though, if she were wearing gloves.

Jones rolled his eyes at her.

"Someday a study is going to come out showing that it's actually good for people to touch things, to feel them, to interact with the environment around them, and that gloves stunt people's spiritual and emotional growth and stability."

She wasn't sure such a study would ever be undertaken, but she was fairly certain that it was important, not just for her, but for the dogs, that she pet them every day.

"I'll take your word on it," he said easily, and that was Jones. He just didn't argue. He was one of those people that were sure enough that he was right that he didn't need to convince the rest of the world. He could stand alone if need be. It was one of the things she admired about him. It was part of the reason he'd done what he did when he opened his vet clinic. Instead of doing what everyone else in the world did, and either become a vet at someone else's practice until he earned enough money to open his own or go into debt even more, to make sure he had all the latest and greatest when he opened his practice, he worked hard with what he had.

"Are you done feeding already?" he asked, noticing the shovel and looking inside at all the dogs who scarfed down their food.

"Yeah. I woke up this morning and couldn't get back to sleep, so figured I'd get out and get started."

She had been awake, that was true. But her bed had been so cozy and warm. It should be since she had every blanket in her house on it, because she'd turned the thermostat down as low as it would go without allowing anything to freeze.

It had been forty degrees in her house when she'd gotten up, but she'd gotten warm once she'd gotten out and started working.

"I see," he said, taking a sip of his own coffee and gazing at her thoughtfully before he looked out at the beautiful view.

That was one thing about her kennels; her home was tiny, just a one bedroom with a miniscule kitchen and a small living room, but outside was a million-dollar view.

He took another sip and turned back to her. "That really the reason?"

She stared. He knew she was having financial difficulty, but she was sure he didn't know how bad it was.

He seemed disappointed and glanced down at his coffee before he met her eyes. "I looked in the barrel last night after I left the house. It was almost empty. You would never leave it almost empty going into the weekend, unless...you didn't have money to fill it."

SIGN up for Jessie's newsletter! Get a free book, access to exclusive bonus content, get fun and funny updates on her life on the farm and more!

A Gift from Jessie

View this code through your smart phone camera to be taken to a page where you can download a FREE ebook when you sign up to get updates from Jessie Gussman! Find out why people say, "Jessie's is the only newsletter I open and read" and "You make my day brighter. Love, love, love reading your newsletters. I don't know where you find time to write books. You are so busy living life. A true blessing." and "I know from now on that I can't be drinking my morning coffee while reading your newsletter — I laughed so hard I sprayed it out all over the table!"

Claim your free book from Jessie!

Escape to more faith-filled romance series by Jessie Gussman!

The Complete Sweet Water, North Dakota Reading Order:

Series One: Sweet Water Ranch Western Cowboy Romance (11 book series)

Series Two: Coming Home to North Dakota (12 book series)

Series Three: Flyboys of Sweet Briar Ranch in North Dakota (13 book series)

Series Four: Sweet View Ranch Western Cowboy Romance (10 book series)

Spinoffs and More! Additional Series You'll Love:

Jessie's First Series: Sweet Haven Farm (4 book series)

Small-Town Romance: The Baxter Boys (5 book series)

Bad-Boy Sweet Romance: Richmond Rebels Sweet Romance (3 book series)

Sweet Water Spinoff: Cowboy Crossing (9 book series)

Small Town Romantic Comedy: Good Grief, Idaho (5 book series)

True Stories from Jessie's Farm: Stories from Jessie Gussman's Newsletter (3 book series)

Reader-Favorite! Sweet Beach Romance: Blueberry Beach (8 book series)

Blueberry Beach Spinoff: Strawberry Sands (10 book series)

From Strawberry Sands to: Raspberry Ridge (12 book series)

Swoonfully Jolly Holiday Stories:

Holiday Romance: Cowboy Mountain Christmas (6 book series)

Cowboy Mountain Christmas Spinoff: A Heartland Cowboy Christmas (9 book series)

New and Much Loved: Mistletoe Meadows (4 books and counting!)

Laughing Through the Snow: Christmas Tree, PA Sweet Romcoms (6 short reads)